THE WELL-BEHAVED TEENAGER (AND OTHER MYTHS)

New Ways to Cope with your Teen's Challenging Behaviours

DR JARI EVERTSZ

Publisher: Inspiring Publishers,
P.O. Box 159, Calwell, ACT Australia 2905
Email: publishaspg@gmail.com
http://www.inspiringpublishers.com

A catalogue record for this
book is available from the
National Library of Australia

National Library of Australia The Prepublication Data Service

Author: Dr Jari Evertsz
Title: The Well-Behaved Teenager (and Other Myths)
Genre: Non-fiction

Paperback ISBN: 978-1-922920-37-9
Hardcover ISBN: 978-1-922920-38-6
eBook ISBN: 978-1-922920-39-3

CONTENTS

Introduction... *v*

1. How Did We Get Here?...................................... 1
2. What Comes Out the Other End 19
3. Teaching Teens to Manage Themselves Independently.... 27
4. Being in Step with the Real World 49
5. Agency.. 63
6. Things That Go Wrong...................................... 79
7. Teenagers' Sense of Self.................................. 87
8. How Teenagers are Wired 107
9. Our Influence.. 118
10. The Bad Behaviours – And How to Respond
    to Them 133
11. Rules for Dealing with the Behaviours.......... 146
12. When Behaviours Come in Groups 153
13. When There Is A 'Whole Situation' 171
14. Encouragement.. 183

Resources 184
Bibliography... 188

INTRODUCTION

PARENTING CAN BE LONELY

When things are going wrong, being the parent of a teenager can feel like a lonely place. It's not like having a child of pre-school or primary-school age when help seems to be everywhere, and it has no stigma attached. When you talk with teenagers' parents, the word that comes up most often is stress. They have a high degree of concern for their children. But feelings of shared pleasure and warmth may have somehow gone astray. They describe rushing around everywhere – not just ferrying kids from A to B, but C to F and L to Z as well. Aside from worrying over their children's school marks and driving them home from basketball at 9 o'clock in the evening, feelings of sadness or anger can dominate for parents. Why? The first part of the answer is that so many teenagers show bad behaviours at home that it has almost become the norm. The second part is that most parents are multi-tasking like never before – and there just doesn't seem to be the space to fit everything in. The third part, is that parents are pouring out their energy and resources trying to get everything right. And they are saddened and hurt by their children's behaviours, which can seem heartless and as if they just don't care. The final component to this difficult equation is that parents are unlikely to reach out as widely (as they would do if a toddler were having tantrums, for example) because they feel a sense of shame and stigma. This can make people hesitate for months before asking for some assistance. And it does feel lonely. People have described feeling like failures.

What's going on? What can have happened to our cute little toddlers and the kids in fourth grade who spent hours laboriously crafting gift boxes and cards telling us we were the world's best parents?

The teenage years bring flaring tempers and slamming doors. Demands alternate with yelling. They refuse to speak and there's little chance of active co-operation or chores being done. Rudeness towards you becomes normal… and their contempt towards you is worse. They seem to hate you while you worry about who they are becoming. They hide things from you. You don't trust them. It seems like your family is not such a nice place anymore. It can get worse. An astonishing proportion of parents report deliberate property damage inside their house, and acts of aggression towards other family members – usually younger siblings and the mother. A 2018 report in Australia indicated that between 1% and 7% of family violence reported to the police is teenaged violence toward parents or carers.[1] A 2003 report by the Sydney Police, though, estimated that between 4% and 25% of all domestic violence incidents were perpetrated by those in the adolescent age group.[2]

In our practice, we have seen escalating stress in families where there are ongoing problems with teenaged children. We have heard from dads who sit in their cars after work, reluctant to start the drive home, and dreading the problems they'll encounter when they open the front door. If a mum is at home all day she may feel trapped and as if no one is helping her. A situation like this doesn't exactly help a relationship, and adult partnerships have sometimes been very damaged or torn apart – and the feelings of loss are immense. Other families trudge on, but their quality of life is poor, battered by the constant shouting and uneasiness inside their homes. The feelings of peace and warmth inside the house have evaporated, leaving tension and frequent clashes. After some months and with no end in sight, 'home' may not feel like a nice place any more. For sole parents, it is even worse: unless they've got understanding families themselves, there's no one to share this with and no one to take over when they've had enough. It can feel like a jail sentence.

How did we get to this? Didn't it use to be different? Surely, our childhoods weren't like that.

Take heart. This is a really common problem – and there are approaches which can help a great deal. You can get your life back and you can feel the love for your eccentric teen again (and they for you). In this book, we look at understanding the developing factors which have brought such big changes to our lives and which we can feel helpless against. We examine the notion of how we build young adults who are strong and positive by teaching important skills in:

- ❖ Managing disappointments
- ❖ Managing emotions
- ❖ Being able to overcome difficulties
- ❖ Connecting
- ❖ Taking responsibility

We will discover the real-world resources that children need as an antidote to the pervasive fantasy world created by social media – such as learning that only personal effort and persistence gain results, and learning that money has to be earned.

We'll take apart the key notion of *agency*, and map out how normal parents in less-than-privileged surroundings can build this in their children. Undoubtedly, not every child has an easy life and so figuring out how to compensate as much as we can for some of life's disadvantages is tackled in Chapter 6. The importance of building a family culture and of finding a supportive resource of community for your teen (at a time when *community* seems to have disappeared) is outlined in Chapter 4.

Not all of us can put ourselves into our kids' shoes when it comes to the un-ending pressures and strange habits of teens and social media. We put this under the microscope (in Chapter 7). Similarly, shedding some light on teenagers' neurological development helps us understand which capacities they develop at different ages… and which they lack (see Chapter 8). To be honest, we also need to get a good handle on the impacts of some of our own behaviours: look this up in Chapter 9. The range and types of our teens' disruptive behaviours – and their impacts – are examined in detail in Chapter 10.

In the final chapters, the structure of key principles and tips, tricks, and strategies is uncovered to help you respond to difficult behaviours in your teenager, in a way that helps you feel calm and knowledgeable once more. My hope is that you will get your mojo back, and feel 10 years younger and less tired than you have been feeling lately. *And* that you will see your son or daughter as the person growing up in the way you'd always hoped for: confident, assertive, and looking brightly towards their future.

One note of caution, though: This book describes techniques which are suited to average-needs children. Youngsters with autism spectrum disorders, conduct disorder, significant depression, or drug and alcohol problems will need specialist help. And so will you, if their behaviours are distressing to themselves, you, or others in your house.

CHAPTER 1

HOW DID WE GET HERE?

Environmental issues aside, our world is becoming a better place to live in many ways. There are laws against sexual harassment and sexual assault that can actually be enforced, and workplace bullying is a no-no. We are learning to respect people regardless of their sexual orientation, and we hold Paralympians on a par with our other athletes, no longer seeing *dis*-abilities where there are physical limitations. We are becoming a more compassionate society, and we take health care seriously. But somewhere along the way, there have been developments that take a swipe at our wellbeing – and this affects children in particular.

Our culture is changing fast. When you were a teenager you probably didn't have a mobile phone, or a laptop, let alone a Nintendo Switch, an iPad, and a games console. The only way of getting in touch with a friend was by calling their house. On the other hand, you didn't have the nightmare of keeping up a social media profile (as a teenager – who might have pimples!). Did you have two hours of homework a night? You were in the minority if you did. You were probably allowed to go to the park or the shops to meet friends, and if you lived in the country you probably enjoyed roaming all over the place, even on your own. Teens were allowed to travel on trains and have babysitting jobs. No one had heard of a helicopter parent.

Up until the 1990s, people thought kids going out in a group was safe and you probably saw your friends face-to-face, for hours at a time. People made their plans at school or by calling their friends at home – arrangements didn't change minute by minute via volumes of texts. Kids probably spent more hours of the day with people of their own age or with siblings than they did in the house with their parents. How do your sons' and daughters' lives compare to the ones that you had at the same age?

In a relatively short space of time, some key things have altered dramatically. Such as:

❖ Beliefs about risk
❖ Access to the outdoors and physical play
❖ Teenagers' belongings
❖ Norms and expectations
❖ Parents' lives

BELIEFS ABOUT RISK

One of the things parents worry about most is their teenagers' potential use of alcohol and drugs. But a look at some of the facts and trends might surprise us.

Rates of alcohol use

The rates of drug and alcohol abuse in our teenagers fluctuate according to cultural factors. While there are no reliable figures for alcohol use in young people prior to World War II, it is known that after the war, when the economy began to expand, alcohol consumption levels rose. It had probably been going up and down across the centuries – in the late Middle Ages, people in northern Europe commonly drank ale rather than water, as water was often unsafe to drink. In the 1830s in Australia, for example, estimated alcohol usage was 13.6 litres per person per year.

During the 1970s, expanding economies and a more liberal social environment were likely factors increasing alcohol usage. But recessions combined with greater health awareness in adults (who tend to control most of the household budget) may have combined to influence the downward trend seen in the 1980s to 1990s. The tendency of teens to stay at home more, combined with more strictly enforced drink-driving laws, may have impacted on the downward trend seen from 2008/09.

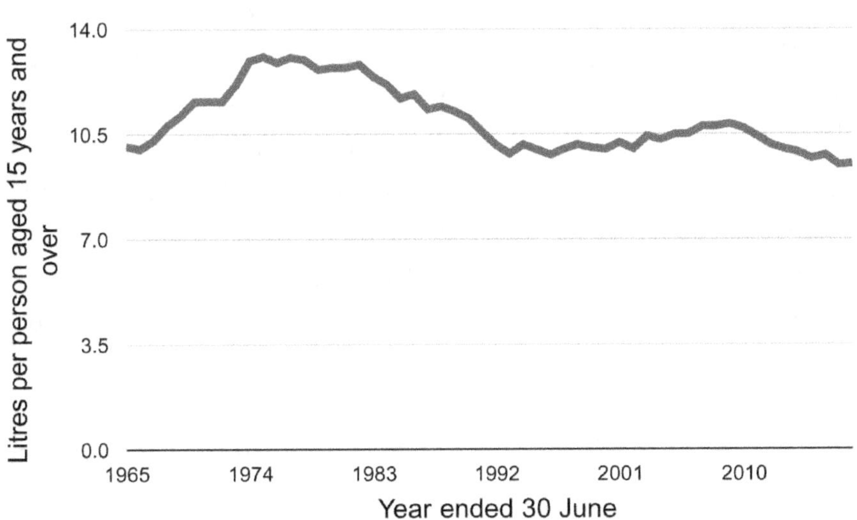

Source: ABS. Apparent Consumption of Alcohol, Australia, 2017-18. Australian Bureau of Statistics, 2019.

A 2018 report estimated that the total alcohol consumed in Australia was equivalent to 186 million litres of pure alcohol, or 9.4 litres for every person in Australia aged 15 years and over.[3] Louise Gates, ABS Director of Health Statistics said:

'This is the lowest annual figure since 1961–62 and it continues the recent downward trend which started around 2008-09."[4]

(You'll notice that there seem to be wide variations in the figures between researchers: we should remember that the figures are estimates and may be gathered differently.)

Illicit drug use

Surprisingly, the main prompt for the sudden increase in illicit drug use from the 1960s was the Vietnam War. This particular war exposed young soldiers to cheap cannabis and heroin when they were under very high levels of stress. Soldiers arrived back in the USA and Australia – and their pattern of use was taken up by the hippy movement, which then spread around the world. After this, the combination of fun, risk-taking, and using drugs to socialise with friends itself became an established pattern. And so as different drugs have become available, they have been taken up by successive generations – from heroin to MDMA to ice.[5] Drug use has remained high overall (though the types of drugs in fashion often change). This may be linked to their small size and extreme portability, combined with the widespread cultural acceptance of their use during large social gatherings amongst those over the age of 18. Recreational use of the 'pills and powder' drugs by the millennial generation appears to be so much the norm at music events, festivals, and large parties, that debate about the merits of pill-testing is currently raging.

Changes in children's lives due to our risk perception

One of the biggest shifts has been that we perceive risk differently – and it has caused a lot of changes. Twenty years ago, children over 11 were thought to be relatively safe in groups and the main risks on people's minds were about physical safety. A common routine for a 12-year-old boy would have been for him to walk to school in the morning, and catch the bus home or walk with a friend. After dumping their school stuff, the boys might go out on their bikes for a couple of hours – though they'd be expected to be back in time for dinner. On the weekends, they would travel even further from home, or maybe go somewhere with a friend's father. They might have gone to someone's work to help with a job, helped with a project in someone's backyard, or made a camp.

There were three key differences in thinking about risk:

1. We thought it was normal for kids to spend a lot of time together without adults.
2. We didn't think that they needed to be under almost constant adult supervision.
3. We thought that danger came from strangers.

Out of these, it's sadly the last that we were most mistaken about. Most of us will know someone who was abused by someone from their family's network as a child. But the differences in our thinking have changed the landscape of children's lives profoundly. Look at a residential street in the afternoon after school, and there will barely be a child outside playing. Few children walk to school: In 1969, 48%

of American children aged 5–14 years walked or cycled to school.[6] By 2009, this had decreased to only 13%. In the UK, the pattern is different, mainly due to a much denser population and the fact that car parking is highly problematic. The UK government's National Travel Survey showed that the percentage of primary school children who walk or cycle in England was 51% in 2017.[7] In Australia, figures are kept state by state. Unsurprisingly, the number of kids walking to school in the state of Victoria, for example, has declined dramatically in recent decades. In the 1970s, almost 50% of Victorian children walked to school, compared with only 20% in 2011.[8]

We no longer see children of primary-school age lounging around the shops with a few pennies in their pockets. Instead, the children are picked up from school (or go to after-school care) and driven home in a car (that means that almost every parent has to have a car.) They go home, do far more homework than we ever used to, and stay in the house with an adult. If they're very lucky they might play outdoors with a brother or sister, or go to the park (but not alone, or with their friends). On weekends, they might have sports training, or go to the mall with their family, and perhaps do something like bike riding or watch a ball game – again, with their family. At most times of the day, children are in the company of adults whether they are at school, at home, or in an after-school activity. If you want to see a real difference, watch news footage or a movie from the 1930s. There are children rampaging around everywhere, and not a parent in sight.

We now perceive that danger is all around (except at home, which ironically enough, is exactly where the biggest danger lies for some children). We have lost our belief in children's competence and in it being "normal" for them to go out somewhere in a group. And this has caused a fourth shift in our perception of risk. This one is about what trouble our children might get themselves into. Our parents probably expected that their children would get into a few minor scrapes or get some bumps and bruises – their worst fears were that a child would be badly hurt in a collision with a car, or abducted by a stranger. Boys, especially, were expected to take part in a few adventures and so they were lectured about the consequences of breaking the law. Parents did worry about their sons 'getting into the wrong crowd.' But as long as their skirmishes were limited to a few silly pranks and there was no one hurt and no juvenile record, it was generally felt that there was no harm done. Teenaged boys rarely seem to meet up with each other now, though: We are carefully sheltering them until they are out of the risk period and so they stay at home battened down – alone – with their gaming consoles.

Social theorists and psychologists see this situation as carrying many losses for children. We expect there to be negative developmental impacts for them over time. Take a look at obesity rates, for example.

Obesity rates

The number of obese children and teenagers worldwide is 10 times higher than it was four decades ago, according to research from the World Health Organization.[9] Overall, over 42% of children and adolescents in the USA are now overweight or obese.[10]

In Australia, the child obesity rates doubled from 1994 to 2014, and in England by 2019, 30% of English children were overweight or obese.[11,12]

Social culture

Children need to learn very complex patterns of interaction to develop their social skills and to gain a sense of who they are. In previous times, they would have had hundreds of hours of unsupervised or lightly supervised contact with children of a variety of ages, but mostly of their own age. Those children would have been free to use their imagination to make up games and activities and to live in their own world for a little while each day. They rarely do that now. The opportunities for free use of the imagination, and for socialisation during activities in environments much less constrained than the school playground, have shrunk. We don't yet appreciate how this may impact upon people's development.

Independence

Roaming around the local area with friends meant that calls were made upon a child's ability to make decisions. They would have had to use the information in front of them to decide which turn in the road to take or which park to go to. There would have been minor glitches and even some significant problems to solve at times. Some they would have tackled together (i.e., co-operatively) and some, alone. This type of task is now almost entirely absent in children's lives; almost every problem-solving opportunity comes either within the household or is set-up by adults in an artificial situation such as the classroom. The 'tough muscle' of independent decision-making is not being exercised at all.

Adventure

Most children love adventure. That is why they love to be slightly scared by their TV shows and movies (in kids past Grade

2, hear the scorn poured on their younger siblings' 'boring' TV shows that have no 'scary bits' in them at all, and the outrage if they are asked to watch the shows with them). But where is adventure now? Peeping out from under ferns in a gully or bowling down the road in a billy cart contraption are thrilling (and really only if there are no grownups too close by). But we have removed these experiences from being on the children's own terms – most activities for suburban children are now carefully constructed by adults. Funnily enough in Australia, if you think about it, there is a right of passage ('Schoolies') where the 18-year-olds who have just finished school are sent to resorts to drink and party together for an entire week – no adults allowed. Suddenly, the gates are wide open, and without much preparation. No wonder the parents are pacing up and down with nerves at night when their son or daughter is gone. It is a big first time for everyone.

TEENAGERS' BELONGINGS

Think back to your childhood. What possessions did you have? Maybe some toys in your room, quite a lot of books, and a bike? It's a very different story today. Children from all demographics often have up to five devices (i.e., an iPad, a laptop and a phone, as well as an X-Box or PlayStation and a Nintendo). They surf the internet freely and contact their friends without their parents even knowing (a bit different to being allowed to use the landline at most twice a week to call a friend – you'd be standing in the hallway with the phone cord stretched to breaking point while you pleaded for 'one more minute'.)

The result is that children, away from face-to-face contact with their friends, have fleeting but constant on–off conversations. Under unending parental supervision, they are much less likely to go out and play but instead retreat to their devices, and there are constant arguments when it's time to put them away. This is a problem. Not only do children feel much more entitled when they have so many belongings that are under their control, but during the span of their childhood they are deprived of thousands of hours of real social contact doing real 'kid' things, and of thousands of hours of outdoor physical activities that stretch their muscles and activate their imaginations. The latter is actually dangerous. We have seen a lot of children with outstandingly poor muscle tone from constant sitting. And their creativity seems to be withering – the jumbo-sized rainbow-coloured drawing pencils in our waiting room are sitting idle these days as children simply ask for a screen to keep them occupied. Children were designed to learn social skills within groups of their peers. While they do this, they are also learning about their own personalities. They are designed to soak up information from their surroundings, and so if they are outdoors they will watch the sky, or examine the composition of a leaf in great detail. Dangling from a tree they can test the limits of their balance and courage (while learning something about gravity). By trying out lots of different physical pursuits, they will soon realise which ones they like while they are learning about how their own bodies function and how to triumph over physical goals. Access in their own room to a variety of different entertainments has reduced these activities for children.

PARENTS' LIVES

It has been a very hard slog since the start of the 20th century for women to be able to claim the same rights and responsibilities as men. And it's not over yet. Still, the societal changes linked to women taking their part in the workplace have been massive – and happening very fast. The biggest changes in workforce participation have taken place since the 1970s. Since the 1970s, the number of women working outside the home has increased a great deal in Australia, the USA, and the UK.

However, women have to put in more preparatory effort to achieve this. In 2020, women were more likely to have a bachelor's degree or above than men in all age categories: for those aged 25–29 years, around half of women (48.3%) and around a third of men (36.1%) had attained a bachelor's degree or above.[13]

In the UK, more women are working than ever before. As of June 2020, more than two-thirds (72.7%) of women aged 16–64 were employed, a figure that has risen from 52.8% in 1971, when the Office for National Statistics began recording this data.[14]

Likewise, women's labour force participation represents a significant change in the US economy since 1950. As of 2020, nearly six in 10 women (57.4%) aged 20 and older worked outside the home (compared with 33.9% in 1950 and 43.3% in 1970).[15]

However, with so much more participation in the workplace, costs have risen alongside the increase in productivity. Very few families can afford to rely on one income during the busiest times of child-rearing. So, a new norm has arisen where both parents need to work away from the home while their children are young (though one might be working part-time). Money is tight and more people than ever are in debt:

Country	Debt level (percentage of income)
Australia	189%
US	101%
Euro Area	95%
UK	125%

Source: BIS, Haver, Morgan Stanley. Morgan Stanley's detailed 68-page report October 2018

So, what we often have is parents who both have to leave for work in the mornings, alongside getting the children up and ready, making lunches for school, dropping them at school or childcare – all before going in to work. This is played in reverse in the afternoons (more often than not with someone to take to an after-school activity) then dinner to get ready, while helping with homework, putting the little ones to bed… parents are lucky these days to get much 'downtime'. They are more likely to be ironing for the next day or washing out lunchboxes until after 9 PM. If one child is younger or doesn't sleep properly, there'll also be chronic and serious sleep deprivation in the mix. There's a frightening impact upon the parents' ability to have any time alone together, or much leisure. If the parents' relationship starts to come apart, you'll often find that one might start to withdraw into gaming or Netflix, desperate for some downtime, while the other stays up even later to finish chores in a quiet house while everyone else sleeps.

NORMS AND EXPECTATIONS

A new feature has emerged for overburdened parents: rather than less being expected of them (because they are so busy), somehow they have come to feel that they need to do *more* for their children. More, in the form of a proliferation of after-school classes, sports, and activities for the school-aged, and Gymbaroo and music groups for the toddlers. And the most extraordinary thing in amongst all of this frenetic parental activity is that we now ask way *less* of our children in terms of chores. Instead, we anxiously provide them with way more possessions than we ever enjoyed, along with electronic devices. My own theory is that this is due to a kind of collective guilt feeling that we have about our children being rushed around and cared for outside of the home. Perhaps we feel they are missing out on home-cooked meals and Mum-always-being-at-home-and-dishing-out-sandwiches. Certainly, parents from further back would have laughed themselves silly at our anxieties. Neglectful or not, they were more confident then. Outside the privileged classes, children might have had one sports activity or a musical instrument to learn: that would have been it – and parents felt fine. They would have been quite happy relaxing on the verandah with a gin and tonic while the children played outside 'somewhere'.

Make no mistake about it, though, it's not just the parents who are feeling the pressure. In our hothouse world, the amount of homework for high school students has been increasing steadily in a context of worry and competitiveness about grades, which was foreign to the average student 20 years ago. An article in *Psychology Today* by Susan Heitler[16] cited increased concern about grade and college entry as the second-highest cause of anxiety-related visits to school counsellors (stress generated by social media being the highest) – noting that anxiety conditions now affect 25% of teenagers, a rate that has been increasing for 30 years and is still on the rise. In 2016, The Sutton Trust in the UK commissioned a report on private tutoring for school students.[17] It found that 41% of school students in London had received private tutoring, while countrywide the figure was 27%. The authors expressed concern not only for the load placed upon children – but at the inequities inherent in expensive tutoring being only available to some.

In the 1980s, there were documentaries broadcast about Japanese children. From their lengthy after-school tutoring classes they would turn to face the camera and explain how concerned they were about their level of achievement and the stresses they were feeling. The suicide statistics for teenagers in Japan would appear on the screen and at the time to us they seemed bizarre. But what seemed alien to the Western world then, lives with us now.

Suicide rates

In 2016, Australian suicide rates for 15- to 24-year-olds had been increasing for 10 years; by 2019, suicide was the leading cause of death among Australians aged 15–24. These researchers found that while the suicide rate for young females has stayed very similar since 1964, for males the rate has increased exponentially (see the diagram).

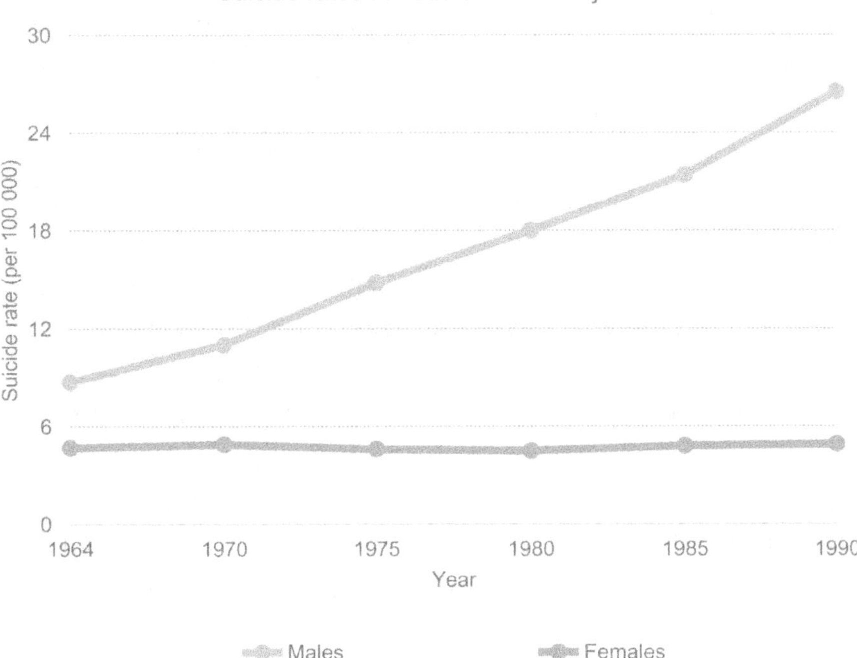

Source: ABS

However, young men tend to use more 'lethal' means than women (such as jumping off high places, hanging, and death by car), so the suicide rates presented here may not reflect the number of suicides attempted and not completed.

We might conclude from our observations about school-based anxiety that academic expectations contribute to critical levels of stress. But the 1999 researchers observed that Australia's high suicide rates in young men could relate to cultural expectations that men, especially, should be tough and resilient (the implication being that they would not bring their difficulties and stresses to anyone). A similar cultural aspect was also observed in New Zealand, the USA, and Canada, all of which have similar suicide rates for young males. This is now felt to be an outstanding problem in Australia and it has given rise to countrywide initiatives such as *Gotcha 4 Life* and *Save our Mates*.[18,19] Meanwhile, the lowest rates for male suicide in the study were in Greece, Italy, the UK, and Ireland – less than half those for the highest countries. It is not presently understood what accounts for these differences.

With all of the busyness we are enveloped by, we are cooking and eating together less, spending fewer hours outdoors and fewer hours when adults and children are able to have leisure time with their peer groups. We are more concerned with our appearances and more worried about money. We are reading, imagining, and drawing less, but texting more. We are all supposed to achieve and 'do better'. Do we really think that these pressures go unnoticed by our savvy children?

TAKE-HOME TASKS

❖ Analyse your child's level of physical activity and decide whether it is enough to make them fit and active – and keep them strong and confident.

❖ Calculate how much time (out of school) that your child spends in the company of other children – preferably a mix between one other and several others. Are they able to experience a level of independence that is appropriate for their age? Can they have little adventures and cook up ideas away from parents' eyes and ears? How many hours a week is your child able to spend developing crucial skills in managing relationships with people outside their family?

❖ How much 'green' (outdoor) time do they have? Time outdoors is essential to develop an appreciation of our environment and to nurture independence. It is also very important for the development of healthy eyesight.

❖ Let them take helpful risks that you feel happy about. Do you want your child to never fall out of a tree or make wonky things in the backyard?

- ❖ Figure out which are the best ways to encourage your child's creative capacities. I don't mean with music lessons or art classes, but time where they try some of their creative ideas out on their own – as kids are meant to do – to discover their own methods and mistakes. They are kids. How are you assisting them to use their imaginations?

- ❖ Share some quiet time with them. Kids often look at this as some of the best times of their week.

- ❖ Carve out some time in the week where you and your partner spend some alone time together. You need it.

- ❖ Have at least half a day a week where you don't need to rush (watch out for your blood pressure and your sanity if you never do this).

CHAPTER 2

WHAT COMES OUT THE OTHER END

HOW DO WE GROW ADULTS?

We are such super-achievers these days. But as we've seen, our fast-driven lives sometimes outpace some of our basic human needs. Maybe because we are all so *tired*; as a group, we are unconsciously outsourcing some of our parenting tasks. Perhaps we're hoping that the values communicated by schools or the messages from our constantly streaming media will be enough to provide examples of maturity to our children. But this means we have dropped the ball when it comes to building adults.

Tribal societies have always had this task figured out. They tend to map out what the expectations of an adult skill set looks like. Then, they provide structures to help the young people get there. These usually include gradually increasing the child's skills in life-maintaining tasks, followed by the provision of challenges and/or initiation (followed by mentoring) for the boys. Girls are more often given steadily growing responsibilities while they are surrounded by a supportive and consistent group of female adults. They may be given formal instruction in the more complex things to learn.

Mundiya Kepanga, a chief of the Huli tribe in Papua New Guinea, commented:[20]

> 'Traditionally, in my tribe, to become a man, teenagers live in the forest for several months under the guidance of many of the elders. It is Westerners who have invented schools with tables, chairs and boards and diplomas. We can learn how to write and read and count and all sorts of things in school. But in my tribe, we had a traditional type of school called Iba Gidja. For weeks, we grew our hair and, at the same time, learned the rules and how to respect others. We learned to live together in harmony and take care of our planet. During this period of initiation, we cut our hair to have a haircut like I still have today on my head. We found feathers to wear for big ceremonies. This haircut signifies that we are respectable people and that we understand our culture.'

The evolutionary biologist Jared Diamond, in his book *The World until Yesterday*, commented that adolescent crises that plague American teenagers aren't an issue for hunter-gatherer children.[21] He reports being struck again and again by how advanced social skills are in tribally raised children. He noticed that people in tribal societies spend far more time talking to each other than we do, and they spend no time at all on passive entertainment supplied by outsiders, such as television, video games, and books. Autonomy is granted to children at a far higher level – but in turn, much greater levels of responsibility are expected as children and teenagers have a vital role to play in the group's activities.

The Western world has taken a long, long time to catch up in providing education for our children. In the 16th century in Europe, only the ultra-privileged received any formal education (which astoundingly enough was very broad, encompassing philosophy, mathematics, ancient and foreign languages, and dancing. Boys were also taught to a very high level of competence in equestrian skills and combat, whilst girls learned languages, music, needlework, health care, and food preserving). Education for privileged girls expanded rapidly after the example set by Sir Thomas More – who set a new precedent for a non-royal person of educating his daughters to the highest level.

Alongside the developments in education, mentoring was part of the system for boys fortunate enough to gain an apprenticeship. Apprenticeship (often called 'indenture' in earlier times) was well established by the Middle Ages. Its cultural importance is reflected in the fact that clear records of this system of passing on skills were kept in Ancient Babylonia, Egypt, Greece, and Rome. The graduates of this long process (then often eight years) derived many benefits: in Europe they became *Master Craftsmen* upon their graduation. When it worked in a kindly way, the benefits of mentoring for growing boys has been very well documented.[22,23,24]

Less privileged children may have been taught their parents' trade if they were lucky enough – and if not – they would have just had to work to survive, as soon as they were able. Up until Edwardian times, working-class children automatically dropped out of school at a very young age to get a job. England first passed a law requiring compulsory education to age 10 in 1870. At the time, this was controversial because it challenged the nation's strict class system. In 1939, the UK Parliament decided to raise the age to 15 (not implemented until after World War II, however). In 1972, the age was again raised – from 15 to 16, following preparations that had begun eight years earlier in 1964.

In the USA, the school-leaving age varies from state to state. Most have a leaving age of 16 or 17, although in several states people can leave at age 14, which is the minimum age for employment. Most young people taking this very early school leaving route will work in agriculture.

In Australia, the education system developed individually state by state. For example, after more than a decade of effort, the Government of Victoria wrested control of the colonial school system from religious denominations, and passed the *Education Act of 1872*. The legislation made Victoria the first Australian colony (and one of the first jurisdictions in the world) to offer free, secular, and compulsory education to its children. Children between the ages of 6 and 15 were obliged to attend school and their education was free. In 1939, the government considered raising the leaving age again to 15, but this was delayed due to the onset of World War II.

The *Education Act 1944* did succeed in extending compulsory education to 15, and this took effect from 1947. On 1 September 1972, the age was raised again to 16 in Australia.

As we can see, it has taken a lot of effort to keep children in free schooling and away from the need to go out and work. But the pendulum seems to have swung a bit too far. In comparison to earlier times, our current teenagers now hold few responsibilities and they are often highly indulged.

The over-sheltering and under-challenging of young people we see at the moment has revealed a new phenomenon: Behold the 'kidults', 'man-children' and 'princesses'. These spoilt and apparently immature young people irritate the heck out of everyone around them with their overdeveloped sense of entitlement (what would the Edwardians have made of them!?). They seem to be unable to take responsibility for anything and their field of vision is narrow: The only person's interests they can see is their own. They are really good at complaining, but this comes along with a frightening lack of empathy for others. Here are some of the things we hear on a regular basis from people aged 18 and above:

'My girlfriend doesn't want me to get a personal trainer just because we're having trouble paying the rent. She doesn't understand how much I need it.'

'Can you write a letter for me because I think I am depressed? I have to go to Court for a fine for my unpaid toll fees.'
'I see. How much are those?'
'$20,000.'

'My mum wanted to buy me the Mazda. I know she's a single parent and everything but I told her, I'm not being seen dead in a car like that...'

'They just don't get me at Centrelink. They don't get what I am interested in.'

'I don't think I'll take a job that has an early start. You know, like 9 AM. I'm not awake then.'

These young people aren't just irritating. They are displaying an astounding lack of insight into what it takes to make your way in the world, as well as seeing other people as mere deliverers of what they want. Their skill levels in decision-making and real-life coping just aren't there. So what is maturity made of? What does it take to make a successful young adult? On our list might be:

Managing Ourselves Independently
- ❖ Managing disappointments
- ❖ Managing emotions
- ❖ Being able to overcome difficulties
- ❖ Taking responsibility

Being in Step with the Real World
- ❖ Learning that a result takes personal effort + persistence
- ❖ Learning that money has to be earned
- ❖ Appreciating the collective landscape of our wants/needs and that of others
- ❖ Compassion every day

Agency
- ❖ Confidence
- ❖ Real-world problem-solving
- ❖ Efficacy – learning that we each have our own talents and contributions

We will look at these in the next three chapters.

TAKE-HOME TASKS

❖ Have a think of what you would like from your child's education. What skills and refinements should they have by the time they are 19?

❖ Which of these are best learned at school and which at home?

❖ What about other skills such as sports, understanding the environment, or practical competencies? In your world, how will these be best taught, and to what level?

CHAPTER 3

TEACHING TEENS TO MANAGE THEMSELVES INDEPENDENTLY

MANAGING DISAPPOINTMENTS

Babies are quite good at managing disappointment. If you watch a baby trying to roll towards a toy and they knock it out of their own reach, they will often just show that wonderful look of baby-puzzlement and then roll off in another direction, fairly unperturbed as they move towards the new adventure. But as we get older and our 'wants' start to emerge front and centre, we need help and constant practice to learn how this can work in harmony with the world. Children are not able to teach *themselves* to wait, or to step aside while other people have a turn at what they want.

Children who are on the verge of experiencing a disappointment will have a strong *want*, a *feeling* that comes with it being thwarted or delayed, and an *uncertainty* about what can happen next. No wonder they 'lose it' when it doesn't work out. It is ok to have strong wants – but they need help to get used to the feelings.

When children take part in lots of activities they gain plenty of experience. Practice helps them to get much more comfortable with the feelings, which then begin to seem less like a disaster. When adults are on hand to provide helpful explanations this adds up to gold: the adult's words become the child's own internal self-talk, which guides them through similar encounters in the future. They re-use and repeat to themselves what they have heard, which soothes their feelings. It helps them to predict a better outcome than their hurt feelings might indicate.

Parents are pretty adept at dealing with the needs of a pre-schooler who is about to have a meltdown, then quickly switching their style to give advice to a teenager. See below as a skilful mum sets a firm boundary for a pre-schooler whilst providing a helpful explanation – and immediately does the same thing (using different language) for her hovering teen who has an urgent 'want'.

Jack (4) – 'Stand back and wait until the others have finished on the climbing net. There's only room for two. Don't worry – you won't have to wait for long.'

Maddy (15) – 'That's a "No" for the party: it'd make the second this week. You know you're no good when you don't get enough sleep. That's right, it's "No". Just remember that your piano exam is more important. You'll feel better when you do well in that.'

It's good to notice that just leaving the child to get his own way doesn't provide anything helpful. Neither does an argument, which doesn't provide them with any help.

With practice, a child's built-in mechanisms help them to get used to frustrating situations. Repeated experiences lead them to recognise when something is just a normal challenge to their emotions. Then, they can take events in their stride and cope without too much trouble. But there's definitely a very soft edge to childhood challenges at the moment – which doesn't help them grow. Students often do not receive marks for their work until they are in the second year of high school – and we're all familiar with the new habit of every child receiving a ribbon in a race. Neither of these provide a clear indication to the child about how they are actually performing.

Have you heard parents describing how their child 'goes nuts' if they don't get to the next level in a computer game? That might help us realise that children need their tolerance for frustration to build up gradually over the years by experiencing real (not virtual) situations. We don't need to protect our children from everyday disappointments. Instead, try taking them along with you in the experience.

Your explanations and your modelling of coping will help them grow into managing disappointments:

'We can't buy pizza until I get paid. Look in my wallet – there isn't enough money.'

'I'm sorry, buddy, that was the last ice-cream.'

'We need to wait until October to buy you a laptop. We can't afford it as Eve needs her braces first.'

'Everyone, your dance marks will be put up in 10 minutes. Your personal ranking will appear in the 3rd column.'

'Thomas, the marks for people going up into the next round were A, A+ and A-. The mark for your essay was a C.'

'Lilly, there isn't a spot for you in Anna's birthday outing. She said she only had space for 10.'

I had a good one of these myself recently. After my car had overheated and was towed to the mechanic's on a rainy winter's night and the next day a small drip turned into the ceiling caving in downstairs, I was explaining the tale of woe to my daughter's friend.

'I would like,' I said to him in exasperation, 'just one week where everything went perfectly.'

Brent looked at me quizzically.

'Well, that wouldn't be life then, would it?' he said, with a grin.

Who was the adult there? We need to be able to appraise life properly and if it's going along ok, to understand that a few wobbles are part of the 'rich tapestry of life' – not have a tantrum (like I nearly did).

MANAGING EMOTIONS

Out-of-control emotions can be like bombs. Our negative feelings seem like emergencies to us – but if we don't manage them well, they can flatten everyone around us. We've all got our list of un-favourites in people who don't deal well with their emotions:

- ❖ The constantly angry person
- ❖ The person who is on a hair trigger
- ❖ The person who gets offended at every single thing
- ❖ The needy person who is always gaining attention for their difficulties
- ❖ The person who is always sobbing into the phone
- ❖ The person whose every difficulty gets spread over the entire house
- ❖ The person who can never be pleased
- ❖ The person who bottles everything up and stays in the corner

Variations in temperament mean that we all have our weak spots. It will probably take you five seconds to list which of your children would be more likely to develop into each of these types. Luckily they've got years to practice, which means they will probably end up a lot better off than some of the adults we may know! Emotional skills build up slowly. Parents are an absolute key part of this increase in skills. If we were to chart the tasks we do for our children's emotional intelligence at their different stages of development, it might look like this:

- ❖ *In infancy:* we comfort, monitor, but at the same time empower children in some areas where they themselves may not think they can succeed (for instance, in settling themselves to sleep, or lying on the floor on a blanket, away from Mum).

- ❖ *During toddlerhood:* parents tend to stand a bit further back to analyse what's going on for their child. Is this a tantrum? Is this tiredness? Being able to tell the difference will change the approach that is taken. At the same time, the parents are building up a good idea about each child's personal style. So, added on to comforting and monitoring are the use of distraction to ameliorate tears or temper, and the use of words to help the child understand what their emotions are. At this stage, drawing the child's attention to the emotional aspects of what they are going through, helps them build emotional literacy. To do this, we have to address them directly:

Toddler is on the sofa with a doleful look on his face –
so Mum says, 'Sad, huh? Want to sit on my lap?'

Toddler is in the kitchen whacking a cupboard door
repeatedly, but she's looking red-faced and hot – so
older sister says, 'Macy, are you tired? Come over here.'

Talking to them directly is a big help as it engages with the child and demonstrates respect: it gets their attention and under these conditions they will pick up the ideas quickly. Young children are very used to being talked over and when they are, they don't listen. So, the approach where a toddler is tucked under someone's arm and borne away to bed while the mum explains to no-one in particular, 'he's tired', won't teach the child who is under her arm very much at all.

Children of *preschool* age really aren't very good at telling what their different emotions are. At first, they are not clear about which ones mean what. If you watch the average child of this age for an hour, you'll see the constant changes in their emotional weather as they go through frustration, delight, concern, worry, upset, and then most likely, pure mischief. But they don't have words for these states and they are unlikely to feel any sort of control. Children don't tend to register their emotions in a verbal sense and so they don't usually identify them correctly. Boys are probably worse at this on the whole. We've noticed that we see a lot of boys – up to age six – who, when provided with pictures of the full range of negative emotions on faces, always identify them as the same: 'Sad.' Spookily enough, some of the adult men who consult with us really struggle to identify and express their feelings, constantly coming up with the same few words to try and describe a range of difficult experiences. So clearly, if children are not taught to know and identify their emotions, they are much less likely to become emotionally literate.

It takes a lot of patient teaching by parents to help a child make sense of their experiences and get to know the finer nuances of their feelings. But when they do, it's beautiful. I was recently asking a five-year-old girl if she'd been angry when her 18-month-old brother had pulled her hair so hard that a clump of it came out, leaving a bare patch. She considered the question for a moment.

'No,' she finally said thoughtfully. 'But I was a bit upset. I did cry. And I felt ugly.'

Parents contribute greatly to learning when they help a child to label and understand their evolving emotions. Once they have experienced and then understood the full range of their feelings, they are open to the next steps: discovering some approaches that gain help and support, and being understanding to others.

Zac: 'Did that make you feel jealous?'
'No. But that brother of mine is just horrible, Mum.'

'Ebony, thank you for not getting angry
when Maeve yelled at you just now.'
'Yes, Miss. She just screamed out because
she was frightened.'

By *Primary school age*, you will have gained a clear idea of each of your children's prevailing emotional weather. This is often related to temperament factors. For example, the child who is often shy is unlikely to be dominant. Rather, they experience a timid and disempowered set of feelings under challenge. Their dominating sibling, meanwhile, will be having a tricky job in remembering other people's feelings as they attempt to bulldoze their way impatiently through many family situations. Both of these response sets lack flexibility and skilfulness and so they are a teaching challenge to their families. A good approach is to take a long-term view and use the many opportunities that come your way to keep helping each of the children to find a more balanced way to cope. Left unchallenged, the child will keep falling back on the way that their vulnerability tells them is the easiest one for them. That pathway leads to a child who is stuck, and who becomes irritatingly one-note in their responses across many situations. They also tend to become addicted to these emotional states, and later on in life will fight others tooth and nail if they try and suggest that a different approach might help! This can lead to a stalemate and to a big reduction in their acceptance by other people once they've grown up. Instead, what will help is continued gentle challenges, requiring the child to gradually push their own coping envelope. If we try not to let them fall back on their usual responses, this will expand their repertoire and allow the growth of a more diverse skill set. Therefore, the shy child can learn to speak clearly in lots of situations (their parents have helped them to practice) and the domineering child can learn that people appreciate their efforts to slow down and respect the feelings of others (their parents will have spent lots of hours on this one!). Parenting is a lot of work over a lot of years.

TANTRUM–THREAT BEHAVIOURS

Children of all ages push boundaries and in doing so they will discover whether cracking it will result in challenge from their parents – or no challenge. As they get older, the resulting manipulation can get more sophisticated... and more threatening.

Five-year-old: 'I want a frozen Coke. I want it now (screaming).'
Mother: 'We're not near the shops, we are at the doctor's office. We can't have one now.'
Five-year-old: throws himself backwards onto the carpet. He yells, 'I want the Coke. I WANT THE COKE. Get it for me NOW, Mum!'

Clinician to an eight-year-old: 'Why didn't you answer your mum just now?'
'She took my iPad away. She knows I won't talk to her until she gives it back.'

11-year-old to her friend: 'If Mum doesn't let me have the unicorn party for my birthday, I'll just cry and cry. Then I won't eat. She always gives in.'

> A sole parent to her neighbour: 'I can't stop my 16
> year-old from stealing food out of the fridge. I just
> can't. Last time I tried he broke a door.'

So, who is training who? Tantrum–threat behaviour is unnecessary. We shouldn't be afraid to displease our children where there are constraints in a situation. In actual fact, humans are built to experience challenges and frustrations at every stage of development during childhood, and these challenges teach us how to manage all different kinds of feelings and to notice other people's needs. Luckily, while we are still children, there is often someone around to help us manage these trials. But the key things are:

a) we have to have these experiences to learn about them
b) people can help us by giving support – *not by taking the problem* away

Try and start early – and avoid the escalation that inevitably follows when smart kids notice that their parents often back down in the face of strong emotions.

OVERCOMING DIFFICULTIES

Whole books have been written on the amazing ways in which people overcome difficulties. Some individuals seem to have an extraordinary capacity for tolerating enormous setbacks and eventually, transforming their lives. Some examples of these 'Super-Survivors' are:

❖ Turia Pitt: Burnt while running a marathon. She became a high-profile mentor, and health and fitness expert.

❖ Malala Yousafzai: Shot in the head by the Taliban at age 15, went on to become an educational activist and the youngest-ever Nobel Laureate.

❖ Nick Vujicic: Born with no arms or legs – now a motivational speaker and international preacher.

❖ Nelson Mandela: 27 years in jail under the Apartheid regime and he not only survived, but went on to change the entire political system in South Africa and become its revered leader.

❖ Professor Stephen Hawking: He did not learn to read until he was 8 and was diagnosed with motor neurone disease at 21. He went on to marry twice, and established himself as one of the world's leading theoretical physicists, thrilling the world with his ability to make quantum mechanics understandable to all.

Understanding such amazing resilience is a complex subject. It's tempting to think that these people are so special, so brilliant, that we could never do what they were able to. If you watch recorded interviews of these people, though, they all come across as warm and intelligent. And also, 'normal'. Three things really stand out to begin with. The first is their ability to appraise their original situation accurately – they had no illusions about their starting points. The second is that they didn't want to stay in those positions. And the third is that they had a vision and a conviction about where they could go instead.

These exceptional individuals do appear to have a whole constellation of skills. But several of these are strengths that can be developed – they do not need to be innate. Setting aside the fact that they all have very high levels of *talent*, there are other qualities that have been essential in powering them along their way. David B. Feldman and Lee Daniel Kravetz studied exceptionally resilient high-achievers in their book about 'Super Survivors'.[25]

One quality in these people is their clarity in knowing themselves. If Nelson Mandela hadn't known that he was a born leader with the temperament to outwit and out-manoeuvre the hugely powerful Apartheid machine, he would not have been able to grow into his eventual role as the nation's leader. Individuals who have overcome profound difficulties to progress to high achievements have a poise and certainty about them as they know very well who they are.

All of these individuals must have had their dark times when they doubted that they would ever escape their own individual prisons. But they also all have the strength within to put negative emotions aside and focus on the step they are working on at the time. This must have taken a huge effort. But it is also a huge strength.

Their planning abilities are of a very high level: They incorporate taking advantage of key opportunities with having the smarts to make course corrections that the rest of us wouldn't be likely to see as necessary. The constant willingness to push the envelope implies a capacity to tolerate almost constant change – something that horrifies normal people! At the end of a difficult day, most of us just ache to reach our home and unlock the comforts within. On many cold mornings, we would most likely prefer that it was actually the weekend so we could sleep in just a little bit longer, and then relax by watching a favourite movie under a warm blanket.

Paradoxically, fantastically high achievers also all have a high tolerance for failure. Not major failures – but the type that you often experience when you stick your neck out and try something people are probably telling you can't manage, or you are not ready for. It's the grasp of probability theory – that each time you try something there is an inherent percentage probability of failure but if you keep on trying with all different kinds of opportunities, you have a far better chance of gaining a foothold than if you never poke your nose out and try at all!

Like most successful people, our 'Super Survivors' (being inherently driven persons who happened to find themselves on the wrong side of life's fortunes) have been willing to devote an incredible number of hours to their chosen vocation. And being intelligent and knowledge-hungry, we shouldn't underestimate the amount of sheer study time they were willing to undertake. Years and years of persistence and thousands of hours paid off, in the context of their skilful self-management.

When you analyse these factors, it looks much less like an act of divine benevolence that powered these people to where they wanted to go. Smaller variants of their approaches to problem-solving would benefit most of the rest of us. Luckily most of us don't need their level of strength to overcome the problems we encounter in our lives. Imagine for a minute how life would turn out if we had *none* of those skills. Luckily, many of us can learn when we need to. For example, if you speak to many people who are aged over 70, you will most likely hear some quite astonishing accounts of setbacks and adversity. That generation would have experienced some difficult times as recent immigrants or people starting out in life with very little. They used determination, vision, and persistence to shape their lives – but they were ordinary men and women.

Our friend Brent was right – normal life is characterised by constant mess-ups, setbacks, and glitches once you are an adult. Therefore, we need to be equipped to deal with them and to build up our skills. And that means, not being sheltered from difficulties.

WHAT ABOUT THE REST OF US?

For a youngster in a normal situation (i.e., they are not experiencing any particular problems), they can get a lot of help from parents who expose them to controlled adversity. That is, a task, hobby, or sport where difficulties are a basic part of it. In many of the colder climate regions of the world such as Northern Europe and the Northern states of the USA, the population is soccer-mad. And it's a *winter* sport. This means that soccer kids turn out in the semi-light of freezing weather conditions to play matches *in shorts*. They will have to wait around on the boundary line, they will fall and get splattered with cold mud, and they will most likely get some scrapes and bruises. Extraordinary. But they talk more about the mates that they have in their team, how much they like their coach, and how nice it is to come home, have a bath, and get warm in front of the fire. Any sport or activity where there are things to enjoy but also lots of setbacks, starts to teach our kids how to survive – and thrive – under these conditions. It means that they don't see periodic difficulties as a catastrophe, but something they are getting used to. They are lucky enough to practice while being supported by adults. It helps if they are able to keep up with their activity over several years – which gives them the opportunity to see how things pan out over time, and to learn and to feel how comradeship and mutual support can develop some amazing problem-solving skills.

LONG-TERM STRUGGLES

Some children on the other hand, are not so lucky. They may wrestle with a problem that isn't going to go away in a hurry. If they don't learn some strategies to cope, these issues can put a permanent mark on them, making them feel very stuck – and angry.

Some of the difficulties that children and teenagers often report to us are:

- ❖ A learning difficulty such as attention deficit disorder or dyslexia
- ❖ A physical issue that affects their capacity in sports
- ❖ A health problem
- ❖ Being 'different' in some way
- ❖ Feeling physically unattractive
- ❖ A family problem that causes secrecy, shame, and isolation
- ❖ Chronic financial stress in the family, which prevents access to opportunities

Children in these kinds of situations are a bit like our 'Super Survivors'. They need a big extra dose of the grit, self-belief, and focus, which are the tools to surviving and thriving in the face of difficulties. Of all these qualities, self-esteem is the one that I'd put highest on the list: you can't move out of the corner if you are crippled with embarrassment and self-doubt. So, it is absolutely essential that these children (who automatically feel isolated) have a great handle on who they are, and what benefits they bring to the world. When they know who they are they can move about un-self-consciously. And if they know what their talents and interests are, they can pursue them with confidence. A funny thing happens when we are confident. We can ask people for more help, take risks and try different avenues in pursuing our dreams. One of the dangers of loneliness and isolation is the strong temptation to remain invisible.

Take the example of a fabulous 15-year-old. She described herself as a 'boho-nerd'. Her mother had an alcohol problem, and she attended a high school where the main girl-groups were totally dedicated to the pursuits of boy-chasing and looking good. Mostly they had great nails and hair. Where was the room for her?

She would sashay into school with her curly hair sticking out and her cardigan slightly askew. She wore glasses, but they merely added to her image. Wisecracking her way around the locker area, she made no secret of her life struggles but instead used them for self-deprecation. Her wit became a solid hit and she found her place – which was happily on the *outside* of all of the main female groups. Everyone felt easy in her company and she had plenty of the boys to hang out with: computer-speak is a gender-less language. Most of the girls ended up going to her with all of their tech and phone problems, and were later able to respect the depth of her intellect. Had she been shy and shrinking into the filing cabinets, she would have had a terrible time.

TAKING RESPONSIBILITY

A friend of mine is a boutique builder. A couple of years ago he announced that he was going to give up having apprentices altogether. I was astonished.

'Why on earth would you do that when you're getting older and you actually need younger guys to take up more of the physical stuff for you?' I asked, mystified.

'Things have changed,' he replied, 'I just can't get anyone who is any good. Even when I'm interviewing them they're on their phones. They want to knock off early and they don't want to do anything hard. I can't trust them to have a go at figuring things out, or to ask a question when they need to. They don't know the most basic things and they are a bloody liability.'

What he needed were apprentices who, even if they were unskilled, could be trusted to give things a go and make reasonably sensible decisions. To do that in an environment where you are the youngest and least knowledgeable takes confidence (not over-confidence). You have to trust yourself enough to make decisions, and ask for help from your senior workmates if you need it. This takes some assertiveness and a basis of a reasonable ability to form judgements (for your age). Plus which, you'd need to demonstrate a good work ethic to gain credibility with your workmates.

Something is obviously going seriously awry in the world of young people and work. One of the first things that young people need in order to take responsibility is an appreciation of the issues at hand. That takes real-world thinking, and the virtual world is not a great preparation. I saw a great interview with the legendary Sean Connery some years ago. He was worried that his son Jason wouldn't understand the more gritty realities of life given his privileged upbringing. To paraphrase, he had told him in exasperation that:

'Life isn't a round of parties on the French Riviera. It's boiling an egg on a gas stove in a cold-water flat in Glasgow.'

Taking part in the mechanics of life is great skills-building for kids. So get them involved wherever you can. If a door is falling off its hinges, get one of them to hold it while you re-drill the holes and screw the hinges back in. It might be uncomfortable to hold a door still, and they might get a bit cold in the draft. If they're like most young teens, they will quickly moan that they are missing something urgent on YouTube and need to get right back to it. Nothing doing. It's important for them to realise that fixing something that is broken takes time and physical effort, and it's not always easy, but that doesn't mean you can't do it.

BE PREPARED

If you get the flu and need one of the kids to rustle up a quick dinner with what is left in the fridge, they will have needed to build up quite a few skills in order to get this one right. If they look in the fridge and see some eggs, potatoes, onions, and lettuce and tomato but they complain that you need to phone for a takeaway, they haven't yet learned these:

❖ Cooking well enough to do without a recipe
❖ Accepting their turn as a helper
❖ Responding to situations calmly
❖ Getting stuck in

Ideally, a 15-year-old could see those ingredients and say:

"Ah. That can be omelettes and salad," and start to prepare dinner without making a fuss. Parents are the ones who need to provide the background skills for the young person to get there. That means building up key skills (like cooking and shopping) and providing lots of occasions when they have taken part in the actions taken to solve a problem. It would be naturally alarming for any child who'd had no experience of anything like that, to try and fix a problem the first time that an adult can't. Families who have a particular hobby or lifestyle have a great advantage here. If you are constantly tinkering with car engines or you go bush camping or you breed animals, there will be lots of opportunities to build up children's confidence and problem-solving skills.

TALKING WITH ADULTS

The other part of this that kids can find difficult is speaking up clearly to adults. It is a shift of role for them to assess a problem and then report this in a way that's not whiny or laced with panicky emotions. If they have plenty of experience in collaborating over projects with adults they will be ready for this role, and able to do it without too much hesitation. Over the years there will be plenty of opportunities to provide practice for your kids. Unfortunately, our recent habits of keeping children conveniently 'in park' with their devices isn't doing anything to help. Children are our amazing little helpers and our own mini-apprentices. What was the motto of that giant construction company?

"Build it Right."

Take-Home Tasks

❖ Identify your child's prevailing emotional 'weather'. What are the vulnerabilities in their coping styles?

❖ Identify which tantrum-threats tend to emerge in your child. Take the opportunity to discuss your thoughts with a family member, friend, or trusted neighbour to plan out how you would like to make some constructive changes in responding to these.

❖ Identify your child's talents. Help them 'own' these… and be able to evaluate them accurately and objectively.

❖ Encourage your child to be themselves – while learning how to show acceptance and respect to others around them.

❖ Take your children along for the ride in solving everyday problems. Let them be helpful to you.

❖ Let your child experience minor failures as they arise – then discuss these with them in a positive and supportive way.

…AND REMEMBER THE KEY TALENTS OF 'SUPER SURVIVORS':

- Knowing themselves and who they are

- Talent

- A clear grasp of their own abilities

- The ability to put negative emotions (such as fear) aside and focus on the step they are working on

- High-level planning abilities

- The ability to take advantage of key opportunities

- Making bold course corrections, which the rest of us might not see as necessary

- Being prepared to use years and years of persistence

- A capacity to tolerate almost constant change as their progress evolves

- The grasp of probability theory: the more times you try something, despite frequent failures, the more likely success becomes

- Hundreds of hours of study time

- Being prepared to use years and years of persistence

CHAPTER 4

BEING IN STEP WITH THE REAL WORLD

Results take personal effort + persistence

DISCONNECT

Have you ever had one of those nights when you've struggled home from work and popped into the oven the gorgeous tray bake that you made so painstakingly on a Sunday evening, heated up the rice that you made with the seeds on the top, and put the rainbow-coloured salad onto the table, only to hear from your sulky teen:

'Nah, I don't want any dinner. I just ate all the spaghetti sauce that was in the fridge with some cheese.'

'What, you ate all of the sauce? But that was for Nicky and her friend to have after they come back here after basketball tomorrow.'

'Oh, Jeez, don't get into me, Mum, alright? It's just sauce. I need to do my homework.'

Never mind about the inner debate you then have to have about how you're going to respond to such breathtaking rudeness, there are several faults happening here. The first is a total lack of appreciation of all the work that you've put in – in their behalf. But if you don't get the children involved in the business of food preparation (or even better – get them to make some meals all by themselves), they are likely to lounge around and be completely unaware of all the effort that it takes to produce a delicious meal. Not many parents spend ages preparing food that the children won't like, or that is unhealthy for them. So you've put triple-effort into the dinner and you'd have a right to feel mighty offended at such a brush-off. If you regularly give your children tasks that they have to follow through to the end (as opposed to just contributing to part of the job), they will build some appreciation of just how much effort goes into important functions. Unfortunately, this isn't easy and probably the majority of parents give up due to the nuisance factor. You know the one: the 'It's-much-less-trouble-if-I-just-do-it' factor. Because really, who wants to face the dramas when a child is attempting to make dinner? The kitchen will look completely destroyed and one part of the menu will be burned while the rest of it still hasn't been cooked, with the whole thing taking three times as long as when Mum and Dad are in charge. But that's what beginners do. If you don't take patience and help them to navigate this stage and then get out the other side, the whole exercise will just be put off – and we're back to the sulky teen who eats his way through the fridge on the slightest whim.

EMPATHY

There's a second part to this conflict, too. And that is a lack of empathy. Notice that the kid didn't blush to the roots of his gelled-up hair, and say **sorry.** Sorry for not waiting; sorry for eating all of his sister's spaghetti sauce she was to share with her friend, sorry for not appreciating your effort, sorry for not caring that you had wanted to eat dinner together. There was a marked indifference. So, while teenagers need Part A of this story (i.e., experiencing the effort of taking a task from start to finish) they also need Part B, which is joining the dots to understand what is dismaying the other person. One problem is that teenagers don't generalise well. That is, if we provide them with an example of something (such as what might impact another person) they don't at first link this to a new situation. This means that they need us to keep on providing examples of how to appraise situations while also bearing others in mind. Their still-immature nervous systems make them egocentric, so they don't always do a good job of seeing the whole landscape. They will usually just see the small section of it which is directly relevant to them.

WHAT KINDS OF TASKS?

You might wonder what types of tasks are good to teach your kids that results take effort and persistence. The answer is: probably a variety of both short and longer projects. They are in need of both a reality check and a real appreciation for the careful putting-together involved in obtaining a result and so the tasks should always involve an element of frustration or need patience. Here are some examples of the quicker ones:

❖ Cooking dinner for everyone – from menu planning to making all of the components, plus laying the table
❖ Shampooing, drying, and grooming the dog
❖ Putting together an item of flat-pack furniture
❖ Mowing the lawn
❖ Sewing a pair of small curtains
❖ Washing both of the family's cars

Notice that all of these require minimal adult involvement. To get a sense of achievement, whoever is doing the task needs to feel the struggle! Make sure that you operate quality control. That is, the job needs to be done carefully and to a reasonable standard. There is absolutely no point in accepting a half-cut lawn with ragged bits all over the edges – there's no real learning there.

BIGGER PROJECTS

Bigger undertakings are very meaningful to young people. If they become involved in something that takes a long time and a lot of effort, it is often like a revelation to them. It feels like a major event in their lives. These big projects need to harness a passion that the child already has, or they'll just feel like a work horse that is plodding along if they have no investment in the activity. Examples of these might be:

❖ Rebuilding a car with an older relative
❖ Training a dog to a high level
❖ Achieving a high level of performance in a sport or in music
❖ Breeding and showing animals
❖ Helping in a renovation
❖ Staging an exhibition of theirs and others' art

- ❖ Writing a book (yes, children can do this)
- ❖ Taking part in a significant welfare or volunteering project
- ❖ Joining a hike or pilgrimage, which is longer than a week
- ❖ Helping in disaster recovery

You'll notice that these bigger jobs usually involve other people, and adults. This is the part that teaches collaboration with people who are not the same age – and it humanises these people and helps to build relationships with them. If you are walking across a mountain range for a week with your father and you see that he is tired and sore, too, it will promote empathy and a desire to help that person.

ANTIDOTE TO FANTASY

The grit and grunt that it takes to persist and complete a big project is also a good antidote to the immense fantasy world that is present in electronic media. With its 'wish, click, and collect' ethos, almost everything seems to be right there, only a credit card's wave away. It's a normal part of children's development to have dreams and fantasies of what they could do if only they wished strongly enough. But that world offers no compensating experience of reality. That being the case, it is we who have to help them understand what it really takes to forge an achievement.

I recently met a contractor specialising in older-house renovations. He had been working in the south of England and had done a very long restoration project for someone who was undoubtedly a member of rock-star royalty. This man, now well into middle age, had a beautiful recording studio attached to his house. Working on the development of a solo album, he was in there every day from 10 AM to 5 PM. My friend Jack could hear whichever riff the guitarist was focussing on, being played and re-played for hours at a time – sometimes days at a time. The development of the new concept took some time before it was ready to take to the studio in London to start being laid down into tracks. I asked Jack how long this practice had gone on for, and the answer came back with a puff of cigar smoke.

'A year.'

That's the difference between a guitar hero and an air-guitar hero.

CHORES

Building up life skills

There is a lot of argument about the notion of chores. Some of us have memories of feeling over-burdened with too many responsibilities when we were younger and so we hesitate to do the same to our own children. Some of us, on the other hand, have got it all together with chores. But many families are so busy running from one destination to another that they haven't paused to figure out what jobs would be good for the children to do. An astonishing 75% of the families bringing their children to us for behaviour problems either give their children no chores at all, or else ask them to do things only on an occasional, ad-hoc basis (which never works out well).

I have to admit that I am really against this. Firstly, it goes back to the issue of teens being over-entitled. Day after day and month after month, it sends a strong message to a child if their parent is constantly cooking food and putting it in front of them and then doing all of the clearing up and cleaning, as well as the financing, taking care of, driving and helping/advising. In a home where this is the case, the children will tend to be sitting on the couch or in their rooms with their screens and they will not even be looking at the parent who is doing all of the work. This sets up a terrible precedent where the children are the 'valued customers' and the parent is merely the worker bee. Valued customers, of course, are entitled to complain – and these ones frequently do! Sound familiar? Then of course, the poor over-worked parent is quite entitled to explode with resentment and give a tongue-scalding telling-off to their lazy and unappreciative offspring. The trouble is, this will be completely ineffective and only add to the climate of resentment. Why? Because actions and experiences speak way louder than words.

Here are some of the benefits of children having regular chores:

1. *Empathy*

We have noticed the most astonishing turnarounds in children who have presented with minor behaviour problems – and where one of the platforms for change has been a regular schedule of jobs within the home. Whereas previously the mother (especially) has said that they do not feel cared for at all by their child – afterwards they have noticed more care and concern coming from their child. We think it has something to do with finally appreciating just how much it takes to get things done. One mum said recently, "Out of nowhere, he asked me if I needed a cup of tea. He has *never* done such a thing before!"

2. *Confidence*

Children are built to gain feelings of confidence not just from what we say to them – but by appreciating their own competence and in feeling accomplished. If they can take pride in a skill, they feel good about themselves. A nine-year-old boy said very proudly to me recently, "I make my mum coffee. Every day. I know just how she likes it." And he flung his arms around the cherished mum he was talking about. Where was my hanky?

3. *Peace*

The atmosphere of a home is different when fairness and help are operating every day!

Derrick (13) and Neale (15) live with their mother Anthea, only seeing their dad for a week in each of the school holidays as he lives some distance away. Anthea works five or six shifts each week at a large hardware store. The boys manage to get to the bus stop on time most mornings and are quite well engaged with their high school, especially since the welfare coordinator encouraged them both to join the lunchtime chess and I.T. clubs. But life at home has not been good.

Let's take a closer look.

Anthea explained that she didn't know whether the problem was her own feeling of sadness, or the fact that the boys were so difficult. She felt she was constantly nagging and shouting at them, with little result. They would not clean up their rooms and would never eat with her. Mostly they ordered in pizza or made toasted sandwiches, failing even to reheat the frozen meals that Anthea had prepared at the weekend. They were usually in their rooms playing computer games and the house always seemed to be in a mess.

The school had phoned once to say that the boys had been presenting in the same clothes for several days and so Anthea would wash, iron, and clean until about 11 pm. She said that she felt exhausted.

Anthea was keen to undertake a review and when she outlined to the boys what she felt had gone wrong, they said they agreed with her. Anthea spoke to her manager and negotiated to finish her shifts two hours earlier for a period of two weeks, as she sorted out the new routines in the house. The biggest success was rostering the boys to cook dinner three nights a week – which they had to do together to help each other. They all enjoyed eating their dinners together and pizza was saved for Friday movie nights! They also liked their 'laundry race' where Neale (hanging the washing out) had to try and beat Derrick (folding the dry washing).

A really important aspect to planning chores is Skills-Building. Just think for a moment – what set of life skills you would like your child to have at ages 7, 9, 12, 14 – and 18? Perhaps make a list of what these look like in your family, at each of those ages. The next question is: how are they going to get there? That is, if you would like your child at age 18 to manage a bank account, travel by train to university, work two shifts at a café, cook dinner twice a week and fill up your car with petrol and oil – will they suddenly gain these skills all at once just because they have left school? Or do they need to build up to these skills over time? When you have decided what skills you would like to see eventuating at each age stage, then you can plan how to help them get there.

Here is a list of possible chores for each age group which we use at the clinic:

Age 2 1/2 - 31/2

Pack toys into the correct box.
Fill a pet's food dish under direction.
Put pyjamas and towels into the laundry basket.
Pick things up which have fallen over.

Age 4 - 5
Take their dishes up to the sink.
Straighten their bed.
Help out with weeding and gardening.
Use a dustpan to pick up crumbs.
Water plant in pots.
Unload *utensils* from dishwasher.
Put milk into their bowl of cereal.
Brush the dog or cat.

Age 6 - 7
Sweep floors with a broom.
Set the table.
Help make and pack their lunch.
Pack their school bag under supervision.
Weed and rake up leaves.
Use gloves to bring in kindling.
Tidy their bedroom once a week, with help.

Age 8 - 9
Load dishwasher or do washing up by hand.
Put away groceries.
Help make dinner (e.g., peeling vegetables).
Make simple snacks for self and others (e.g., fruit, cheese, and crackers).
Wipe up spills alone.
Groom a pony or clean tack.

Age 8 – 9 (continued)
Wipe the table after meals.
Make own breakfast (e.g., toast, cereal, fruit, yogurt).
Make toast.
Make sandwiches.
Mop the floor.
Clean people's shoes.
Provide the food or water for a pet or farm animals to
a regular schedule (e.g., before breakfast every day).
Hose the patio.

Age 10 – 12
Unload the dishwasher or put away
hand-washed dishes.
Fold laundry.
Load and start the washing machine.
Wash the car.
Do the vacuuming.
Make a cooked breakfast for everyone.
Make tea and coffee correctly.
Make toasted sandwiches.
Help with tasks for younger siblings (e.g., feeding,
changing clothes with adult in the home).
Change their bed sheets.
Fully tidy their bedroom weekly.
Fetch in wood.

Age 13 – 15
Do the laundry.
Organise the laundry into each person's belongings.
Cook a simple meal (e.g., pasta and home-made
sauce with salad; omelettes; a stir-fry; meat loaf with
mashed potatoes and green beans; baked fish with
vegetables).
Pack school lunch for themselves and the other
children.
Do ironing.
Clean the kitchen.
Chop smaller wood pieces.
Stack the woodpile.
Take responsibility for a younger child for an hour.
Make up and light the fire.
Mow the lawn.
Do a small shop for groceries.
Clean up outside.

LEARNING THAT MONEY HAS TO BE EARNED

At the moment, the Western world is not set up in a way
which automatically teaches children the value of money…
that is, that it has to be earned. Several things contribute to
this. One is (as we've mentioned previously) that children
have a lot of things *and are provided with* a tremendous
amount of things for their comfort and consumption,
including the ferrying around that parents do, the waiting

around during sports lessons, the ironing of uniforms late in the evening, parents leaving work early and then having to write reports well into the night, etc. Parents in our times have a strong urge to provide well for their families (as they probably always have done) – but a difference now seems to be that they want to look as if this is all effortless. It's the old analogy of the duck gliding around serenely on the water while underneath there is frantic paddling going on. And at the same time as we are working frantically to get things together for everyone, the kids are often just sitting on the sofa hooked on the iPad… which your hard-earned money has provided for them.

So how can we reconcile our desire to feel that we are doing well, providing for our children, and not wanting to guilt-trip them – with providing them with an unfolding appreciation of how money has to be earned?

CHAPTER 5

AGENCY

WHAT IS AGENCY?

Agency is a very important psychological concept. In a nutshell, it means that a person feels that they are effective in the world. They have an accurate *but empowered* sense of who they are and what they can do. A large number of children do not have this. They either feel hesitant and nervous in novel situations – or they are plain used to adults doing everything and making everything happen – or they may be *over*confident and have a grandiose and yet unrealistic idea about what they can influence and bring about.

What does agency look like in different age groups?

Age 5

I can't see my dad. Mum said that if I can't see her or Dad at the mall, I can go and talk to a lady who has a uniform or one who is in a shop. I am scared, but there's the jewellery shop lady!

Age 7

I know what is happening to Mum. She is having a hypo, she has told me about those. I have to pour a juice box down her throat, then turn her on her side. Then I can call the lady at triple-0. I have never done that before.

Age 9

I'm having that feeling again. My coach says it is an anxiety attack. I hate how it feels, it is horrible. But we practised me breathing slow and focussing on the track ahead. When I'm out there I know which lane I want.

Age 11

They have forgotten that I can't get my chair out there. I don't think they realise they have left me behind. I will take the other pathway to the middle level. I can practice my spins there and then they'll see me!

Age 13

Rusty's gallop is a bit fast but I think I can make him pay attention. When we come out of the woods I will sit down hard and straighten my back. When I do that, he usually listens to my voice. After that it's over the ditch!

Age 15

Amelia is drunk as hell. I saw about this in a movie.
Let's get her outside away from everyone and then get
her to drink some cold water. She'll probably throw up
but she's lucky she's got us looking after her!

Just imagine what would happen to the children in each of those situations if they didn't feel they could handle things.

Agency, as you can see, is not simple – it is made up of many components. What was in use here?

- ❖ *Coaching*:
  In each of these situations, the child has been coached or rehearsed the scenario (these were not situations which needed the child to extrapolate into an entirely unexpected scenario).

- ❖ *Information:*
  All of the children have enough information to use the resources they have, to deal with their situation.

- ❖ *Capacity:*
  The actions they needed to take were a match for their own capacity.

- ❖ *Calmness*:
  .... this is linked to:

❖ *Practice*:
It doesn't seem likely that any of these kids had never experienced problem-solving opportunities before. Rather, it looks as though they have previously been supported to tackle tricky things.

❖ *Effective self-talk:*
Notice how the children seemed to talk themselves through what they had to do. This is a crucial skill.

❖ *Mastery*:
All of this preparation has evidently provided each child with the sense – even under adversity – that 'they have got this'.

Children would be at an advantage if they felt a sense of agency more often than not – it can accompany them through many parts of their day:

❖ Travelling to school
❖ Arriving at the lockers
❖ Preparing for classes
❖ Dealing with changes of rooms or classes
❖ Interacting with peers
❖ Advocating for themselves with adults and making their needs known
❖ Dealing with peer problems or bullying
❖ Managing when something goes wrong with their work
❖ Sport (often a place where anxious kids feel horrendously embarrassed)
❖ Taking the bus
❖ Meeting friends at the mall
❖ Team sports after school

One of the things about agency is that it connects a child to their wider environment. These are not kids who are moping around inside the house or hiding from the world in their rooms. They have a sense of their place amongst everything, and a willingness to take part whilst understanding how their world works. What's one of the top-five risk factors (often not spoken about) for both juvenile delinquency and damaging levels of substance abuse? *Lack of engagement with their community.*

CONFIDENCE

Confidence and agency are closely related. When someone is feeling confident, they are not so much focussing on how effective they are: it is more that they feel:

"I am ok here. I can be here; I am as good as anyone else here, and I can probably keep up with doing what they do."

Born confident

Lovely examples of confidence can be seen in pre-schoolers. Granted, some of them may be displaying early signs of anxiety (such as lowering their gaze to new people, hiding behind the parent, clinging and refusing to take part). However, *most* of them are completely unself-conscious. It's a wonderful thing to walk into a preschool and see the little ones busily going about their play – pouring water and organising each other at the sand tray, chatting and laughing, then suddenly running outside to swing on a tree and run in circles. It sounds like a cliché, but this is a stage of life where most negative events, increasing concerns and feeling excluded, have not happened yet. So, the children are being their natural selves. It's probably no coincidence that preschool children are encouraged and supported more than they are told what to do or left in large groups where they may not feel capable. But whatever the things that take confidence away, it is a joy to watch a four-year-old engaged in social play, or a two-year-old striding towards his mother with a handful of flowers, full of confident self-importance.

If you think about it, confidence in yourself is the one thing that you can take everywhere you go. It is just as relevant at a society high tea or stepping off a boat on a choppy river. But what is it made of?

Damage

Certainly, confidence implies a lack of damage to oneself. Damage to confidence can come from many sources and it is a very complicated matter. Some children, for example, can stare at a child on their table at school who is in the habit of saying malevolent things, and just go back to their drawing. Others would become tearful and start to avoid their group, and their parent would have to get involved to try and persuade the teacher to change things around. Of course, many people experience significant issues in their lives that mortally damage their confidence.

But think of it this way: there is a hammock in the trees. That's our confidence. We want it to stay up high, but things keep pulling it down. *So in order for it to stay high, there needs to be something that keeps on pulling it back higher up in the tree.* The things that keep pulling it back up can be varied but they have to work for that particular person. For some, it is their own rubber-ball personality that just bounces back hard whenever someone tries to pull them lower. For others, it is their exuberant group of siblings who provide lots of fun and gusto and mucking around.

And for others, it is the practical parent who is straight onto instances of wavering or hesitation. One other thing to remember, though, *is that the forces pulling the hammock back up need to be equal or greater than what is trying to pull it down.* So if the negative forces are major, it will take a lot (and probably a combination of things) to get that hammock back where it ought to be. This pulling and pushing probably explains why older children are more likely to be less confident than their toddler cousins: there have been more opportunities in their lives for things to go wrong. Therefore, damage is something we need to keep a look out for and it needs thought and effort to try and put it right.

A positive self-view

One of the important ingredients to confidence is a positive self-view. That is, a feeling that we are doing ok; that our values are good, and that the things we are interested in are ok with us. This isn't just a superficial thing – it runs deep. You can see it in a child who is smiling gently even though they are in the middle of a group of people who are completely different to them in some important way. It doesn't matter what you are good at or what you like about yourself: *what matters is that it is ok with you – through and through…*

Take this example: Two sixteen-year-old girls are interviewed about themselves and what makes them tick.

Girl 1

Well, I live with my mum and that's nice because it is quiet. I love maths and music – especially my violin. I like to read but don't make me cook because I am rubbish at it. Haha. Also – Mum tries to make me garden but I hate getting my hands dirty. You won't catch me out there much. And I hate big dogs like German Shepherds. Erk. They give me the creeps. I think the future for me will definitely be something to do with peacefulness and music – and that's great because I love it.

Girl 2

Yes, our house is noisy because there are five kids. I am the oldest. It would be spooky if it was quiet. I'll tell you straight up that I'm no good at things like maths and books and I hate music at school because I'm just tone deaf. People at parties try and make me sing 'cause it's funny! (Laughs.) But actually, I am a pretty awesome cook. My parents gave me a bit of the garden and you should see the veggies that I've got growing. They go straight into what I am cooking that day. And I go everywhere with my dog. Come here, Bazza! He is a Belgian Shepherd. Look at the size of him. But yes, cooking is going to be the way for me.

You've got it. These two girls are diametrically opposite to each other. But they are both delighted about what they like, and couldn't care less about the things they are no good at. Luckily, neither of them seems to have heard of that pernicious destroyer of self-confidence: negative comparison of one's self to others.

MORE ABOUT PROMOTING AGENCY

In the first part of this chapter, we looked at the sorts of activities that promote agency. Confidence is a great starting point, but there needs to be hands-on experience for a child to engage effectively with a problem – or an opportunity. How often have you seen a child hanging back in an unfamiliar environment, refusing to take part as it is all too new?

Child 1

Mother: 'That's right. It's a barn dance and it is in a real barn. See the hay? If you want to take part you go over there and we will find one of those people for you to partner with.
It's a simple square dance.'
Child: 'Is it a bit like what we did at church that time?'
Mother: 'That's right. Except here you go around and you don't change partners.'
Child: 'Is it ok for me to dance with a grownup?'
Mother: 'Sure, sweetie. I am right here watching and you'll see that the people are all neighbours that we know.'
Child: 'Ok!'

Child 2:

Child: 'I don't like it here, it's yukky. Why is there all that stuff on the floor?'
Mother: 'Well, it's a real barn. Now, the plan is for the children to go and partner a grownup for a dance. Go on, it's over there.'
Child: 'Whaaat? I don't want to dance with a grownup. What's going on? I don't get it. I want to go home.'

Child 2 has not only had no preparation for this, *but it is also too unlike anything she has come across before.* It's important to remember that children do not generalise skills well. That is to say, if you teach them something in one situation, they cannot necessarily apply the skills to a very different situation. Child 1 made the links that he had done something that looked similar, somewhere else. His mother also spoke to him in an informative way. Together with an adequate level of self-confidence, it was enough to make him happy to give things a try.

TAKING PART

Outside of their family, the best place to see children operating confidently is in a large group setting where there are lots of different age groups, some familiar activities or routines, and a repeated experience for the child of being there and feeling part of it all. Such places are very diverse. They could be the soccer club where the child and his older brother have been going for two years, and where there are regular events and dinners and a hands-on job for everyone; or the Somali Community Centre where the child has always seen his mum and his aunty joyfully cooking for large events and where there is always noise, music, and laughter; or it could be the church where kids have their kids' club… right after they have spoken part of the readings and sung their special song in front of everyone.

The important things are that they go regularly and over a long period of time, they see people relating and solving problems together, and they get to participate with people from all different age groups.

Community is very, very important. If children don't have anything like this, then they may well exist in relative isolation and not experience either helping diverse others, or being helped by all sorts of people. There may be a community feel at their school, but it may well not be personalised enough to have an impact. And the sense of connecting to people of all different ages is crucial. It sounds a bit like Hilary Clinton's favourite saying:

"It takes a village to raise a child."

Here are some of the education components of a community setting:

- The child feels that they are a part of something
- They develop respect for people of different ages
- They get used to communicating easily with people of different ages
- They get to experience being around a parent but not needing to be right next to them
- They get to express themselves freely in a large group setting

- ❖ They get to celebrate with people other than their family
- ❖ They get to feel useful
- ❖ They get to experience noise, colour, and activity
- ❖ They experience the pleasure of putting effort into something that is not of direct benefit to them – it is for everybody
- ❖ They develop real relationships with supportive people they would not otherwise have met

COMMUNITY. COMMUNITY. COMMUNITY.

I CAN'T, DON'T MAKE ME

Teenagers certainly go through a period of about four years where they are: (a) reluctant to do things with adults and (b) reluctant to do anything which is outside their 'approved zone' (read Comfort Zone). With seesaw emotions, uncertain self-esteem, and fatigue at funny times of day, they often baulk. There are other reasons why there is a strong tendency for them to shy away from adults – more about that later – but there are many pitfalls to this one. If you leave them alone in their rooms for long periods of time, then you don't know what sorts of activities are happening on the internet. Further, you are not only validating their tendency towards avoidance of the broader social scene, but each extra hour they spend successfully avoiding friends and family, they are reconfirming avoidance as a strategy for coping and their skills at interacting are potentially withering.

There is a balance to be struck, of course. Teens are trying to find out who they are, and their preoccupations do not sync well with the (apparently) incredibly unexciting experience of eating cake and chatting with an auntie. They need adequate time spent with peers and in their own imaginations. But beware – if they are left to 'do it their way', those aunties can suddenly realise they haven't really spoken to their nephew for a good couple of years….and they don't know who he is, anymore. It is very important for young people to have people around who know and understand them so that they feel safe and held by a wider family. When they are out of sorts with you and with themselves, you really don't want them feeling that there is no one else in the world to turn to.

IT'S A FAMILY THING

Teens do better if they can be involved in something with their adult family members. This is amazing for bonding together as well as for helping them to grow their skills: and you don't have to talk much – which they often hate. Ever noticed that when you are driving alone with one teen, their first impulse is to reach for the radio and turn it up loud or put their earphones in? No danger of having to talk to an adult, then! Here is a list of some activities teenagers have told us that they enjoy doing with their family members:

- ❖ Stock car racing
- ❖ Logging
- ❖ Fixing cars
- ❖ Building things
- ❖ Fixing things around the house
- ❖ Dirt bike riding
- ❖ Mountain bike riding
- ❖ Golf
- ❖ Horse riding

❖ Work with metal
❖ Embroidery
❖ Droving
❖ Cooking
❖ Cake making

❖ Dog shows
❖ Poultry shows
❖ Truck deliveries
❖ Model planes
❖ Surfing

…and of course, any kind of sport that you all enjoy.

As long as they are felt to be fun, all of these activities have the power to bring you together in a positive spirit rather than a reluctant one. That can seem like an otherwise rare opportunity with a teenager. They can learn how to challenge themselves and grow new skills, and it gives them plenty to talk about while you are driving home. That's a big increase in connection compared to them staying in their room the whole time.

BUT I HATE WHAT WE DO

Beware of the impulse to construct something which you do most weekends… and which the children don't really like. It can result in this:

'We go to the cabin every weekend pretty much. It's by the lake. But it's boring. I don't like it, really. In the winter, it's freezing up there – there is a fire but it's the only one, so my room is extra cold. We don't do anything that I would like as Dad's passion is fishing and I'm the boy so I have to go with him, every time. That'll be every Sunday, almost all day. It takes so long. I can't say anything to him as his hobby is the reason why we go. I really miss all of the things my friends are doing back home. Actually, I hate it.'

EFFICACY

What are you good at? And how long did it take you to discover that? We are all really helped by finding that we are just darn good at something. It gives us a new place in the world, a brightness in our step, and some confidence to look the world in the eye. High school is the place which is supposed to give us an array of new learning topics so that we can find the ones which we like – but the primary school period is a great time for discovering talents. It doesn't matter whether these are fixing things around the house with Grandpa or making cakes. If children can discover something like this while they are still young they can push forward with it. They discover how it can mesh with parts of their personality – and this helps to create a strong feeling of identity.

'I like writing fairy stories. It's good because I can do it in my room on my own. I can take my time and think the stories out. Then I do the illustrations. That's the best bit! When I show my friends or my grandma, they are amazed. It makes me happy and I do feel proud of myself when I look at the drawings. Mum said I could take them anywhere and people would like them.'

'I like rebuilding engines with my dad. We can spend hours out there. He is starting to let me use more and more tools. It's awesome when the engines go back

> in and they work. You should hear the noise in the workshop! I've also discovered that I'm pretty good at fixing things in the house, especially if Dad or Grandpa is helping. It's good really as I'm slow with reading and maths, and at school I spend so many hours feeling dumb.'

ANTIDOTES TO LOWER ACADEMIC SKILLS

The second story is a bit of a giveaway. If we feel good at something, it helps to cushion us against the ups and downs we experience out in the wider world. If you think back to your childhood, the odds are that there was something that felt humiliating for you at some stage. It might have seemed that it was going to crush you at the time. We all need a counterbalance to that – a corner of our world which still works when everything else is going wrong. And in this case – a corner of ourselves which we know still works when we are being told that we are no good. Remember the hammock? The more something is pulling down our self-esteem, the more something else needs to be supporting it. This is especially true for children who have some struggles with learning in the classroom – they can experience 'feeling dumb' for six and a half hours a day, five days a week, in front of their friends. A great skill and confidence in some part of ourselves is essential for real well-being.

CHAPTER 6

THINGS THAT GO WRONG

OUR LIVES CAN GET SERIOUSLY MESSED UP

We are very lucky if something doesn't go astray with our life plans. We almost never see disasters coming and we don't think it can happen to us, and if it happens, we sure wish it wasn't us. Some issues in particular cause significant problems for the children of the family. They may cause some of the following kinds of damage to the family environment:

- ❖ The family function goes into 'Emergency Mode' … and keeps on functioning like this.
- ❖ Shame and degradation of the family's values and culture.
- ❖ Isolation – being cut off from other families, no longer feeling part of things.
- ❖ Abnormal ways of relating within the family.
- ❖ An unsafe environment at home, or outside of the home.
- ❖ People hiding from the person or people who are the greatest problem.

FAMILY FRACTURES

The types of situations which can cause this include:

- A problematic divorce
- Stressful access/separated parenting
- Low income and insecure housing after divorce/ family violence
- Sudden reduction in resources following illness or retrenchment
- Isolation of a family (especially a sole parent family)
- Families interstate, families overseas, broken links with families
- Dislocation from originating culture
- A poor relationship between the parents (conflict, disengagement)
- Alcohol and drugs in the house (a parent/older child)
- An older child who is disengaged/contemptuous
- Family violence and abuse
- Chronic illness
- Mental health issues in a family member

The disruption of a family's culture together with elements of struggle and fear and a sense of desperation makes growing up confidently very hard. So, what types of damage can occur for the kids, and what should we look out for?

UNSAFE ENVIRONMENTS

Poverty and struggle are bad enough, but even more damaging are situations where there is something toxic or unsafe within the home:

- ❖ an older child with a drug issue who regularly frightens people
- ❖ a violent adult partner
- ❖ someone who is sexually unsafe
- ❖ someone with the volatile behaviours associated with a personality disorder that other family members just cannot manage to contain
- ❖ someone who drinks and is violent

These are the types of circumstance which make children hide within their own houses. Teenagers in this situation are much more likely to leave home. Have you ever wondered what produces teenage homelessness? Teens leave because 'out there' looks safer than inside their own family homes.

ADVERSITY VS TOXICITY

Humans are very resourceful, and we can adapt to many types of changes. If you are reading this from the USA or Australasia, for example, it is likely that whole sections of your family left where they were living and took the huge journey to another continent. Most of these families ended up eventually better off for having done so. So, periods of challenge and adversity which have the clear goal of producing betterment, may not be crippling. If you are a person with vision and determination you can use straightened circumstances to spur you on to greater things. But that is the key: to be able to maintain your vision and self-confidence and have the energy and focus to keep going. It works best when better things are visible just around the corner. That is why we espccially have to watch out for situations which are *not* like that and which can cause the following:

❖ Chronic withdrawal
❖ Depression
❖ Lack of confidence
❖ Loss of feelings of agency
❖ Loss of self-belief
❖ No idea in the child of what they are good at
❖ Loss of connection to a community
❖ Loss of engagement with learning
❖ Acting-out behaviours
❖ Loss of identification with positive role models
❖ Identification with negative role models

A lack of safety, a toxic home environment, or badly disrupted home routines or relationships need to be temporary. Children and young people just cannot develop in a positive way otherwise. However, if you find yourself in a situation where there are real difficulties but you can keep key aspects of your family and your child's identity intact, help is at hand for your child to develop well in the midst of circumstances that are less nurturing than you would like.

As we've said before, children feel greatly encouraged by being part of something which has an ongoing sense of community. It is a great irony that disaffected boys (especially) who feel isolated and who run off to join gangs or outlaw motorcycle clubs are met with rules and restrictions which are far more onerous than they ever had at home! But what those 'gang' environments do offer is a sense of belonging and a feeling that you belong to a community that knows what it is doing.

Better places where vulnerable kids can find this kind of 'home' include:

> ❖ A generous and welcoming church/mosque/temple
> ❖ A club or sports club

For clubs to fulfil this role, they need to have a range of activities (i.e., not just a lesson each week). There also needs to be lots of contact between the adults and the children; active involvement of the children as helpers, regular occasions where people eat together, and longevity – so that the child knows they can go back year after year. This might be a soccer or basketball club where parents carpool and where everyone gets together for brunch, a Landcare group which travels a lot to plant trees and repair creek banks while sharing sandwiches, or a chess club where younger members are mentored and everyone gets together for an evening dinner.

The older brother of a man who had passed away suddenly became a mentor for the man's son (his nephew) tutoring him in the ways of life and of their family's religion. They met twice a week for dinner and conversation and the boy was picked up and accompanied to the mosque every week. The growing boy developed an interest in a medical charity and his uncle is now helping him to travel and raise money for his cause.

One grandmother drove a round trip of over 100 miles (160km) from her dairy farm every week to see her granddaughter and take her to ballet. Costumes would be made and mended and many conversations had in the car on the way to practice. As far as we know, this continued for over 6 years.

Feeling part of something is good, but feeling individually cared for by someone from a positive environment is a different kind of powerful stuff. Amongst the children under stress who attend our clinic, the lucky ones are those who nominate a favourite 'extra' person in their lives. Children often speak warmly and at length about a grandparent, aunt, or uncle whom they feel understands and loves them. We have seen many grandparents and extended family members who play a key role in children's lives:

Children love the regularity of repeated visits to a loved extended family member. Many kids love visiting Nanna and are thrilled to look forward to their regular activities of baking cupcakes or walking the dogs in an environment that is somehow less stressed than home. Sympathy develops and activities take place in a more measured way in such a peaceful setting. Children often tell us that their Nan is the person who understands them the best and who never tells them off! (Of course, outside of the hurly-burly of a house where homework has to be done, there isn't enough time or money and people always have to be somewhere, there isn't much *need* for tellings-off! But what matters is that the child gains an experience of a tranquil environment where they do activities that they like whilst experiencing warmth and connection with someone who matters to them.)

The growth of skills is another helpful platform for children who are experiencing stress or disadvantage in their lives. The keys here are having someone safe who shares the child's strongest interest and who has the facilities and the knowledge to provide regular and long-term activities.

One little boy lived alone with his mother who ended up severely injured at work. Restricted for activities outside the home, the little boy also battled dyslexia. His grandfather lived in a regional city and every school holidays he came to collect his little grandson, who loved to help out in grandfather's farm maintenance business. The lad grew skills and confidence and a sense of pride which helped him to keep his head above water at school. One day he will also be a great farmer and buildings 'fixer'.

A little girl with cerebral palsy had an aunt who travelled around to different clubs as a horse-riding instructor. Her niece loved to go with her and did a great job at riding. Listening in to her aunt's theory lessons built up her knowledge so well that she ended up teaching theory to the 'littlies class' herself.

In summary, what kids need when something is disrupting their home lives, are these:

❖ A community or 'second home' where they feel they belong and where links are strong and lasting
❖ Safe adults whom they form direct relationships with
❖ Plenty of discussion and mentoring by the adults
❖ A platform for a strong sense of identity
❖ The growth of positive values
❖ The growth of skills

❖ The growth of self-valuing
❖ Contributing to the welfare of others

Kids who are stressed only have three places to go: Acting-out, withdrawal, or dissociation (i.e., mentally 'going somewhere else'). These may feel like protection to them, but they are dangerous and offer no growth whatsoever.

There is an African proverb which says, "The child who does not feel the support of the village will burn it down to feel its warmth."

CHAPTER 7

TEENAGERS' SENSE OF SELF

Many of us feel very little connection to the sorts of lives that teenagers are living now. While we might go along with or manage some of the things that make us uncomfortable, we don't really know what it's like to live as they do. How many times have you found yourself saying:

- ❖ 'We managed without all of your technology when I was a kid. Can't you entertain yourself?'
- ❖ 'How many products do you need in the bathroom? What's wrong with your hair without all that stuff in it?'
- ❖ 'Insta-what? Stop that. Why do you have to send photos of yourself anyway – you've just seen your friends this afternoon.'
- ❖ 'No, you can't take your dinner into your room. Come and eat with us. My dad would never have let us eat anywhere except at the table in our house.'
- ❖ 'No, you are not having Volleys. Have you seen how much they are? Normal tennis shoes from the mall are good enough. Stop fussing.'

❖ 'Get off your phone. We are here at Grandma's for her birthday. It's extremely rude to be looking at that thing all of the time.'

❖ 'What are you worried about – you're a perfectly normal looking girl. Can't you just disconnect from all that social media stuff?'

Life has changed so much that some of the most important aspects of our teens' lives are things we haven't experienced and don't really understand. We tend to think that our kids are much more self-absorbed and rude than we were, but let's stop and consider some of the seemingly immovable influences in their lives.

CONSTANT ACCESS

Teenagers feel that they have to be constantly up to date with what is happening in their peer group, and constantly available in case they miss something. To stop would be to risk suddenly being on the outer. There's a lot of fear here – as if relationships and being valued by others can change in the space of hours. Bullying and exclusion have taken on different forms – and these may be completely out of the line of sight to adults, existing in the mysterious and ever-changing cyber space platforms – whichever is flavour of the month.

CONSTANT SCRUTINY

Can you imagine what it must be like to be a teenager (with all those well-known insecurities) and to feel like you have to keep your best, most buff appearance up across all platforms, all of the time? Your competition is not just from your immediate friend group (and that's what it can be like

– competition), but the entire group of their friends, as well as the sea of people who can suddenly appear on social media. Teens are living their lives feeling pretty exposed and on public view: it's not uncommon for them to have social media 'friends' in the hundreds.

LACK OF BALANCE

When you were a kid you probably had some alone time walking home from the school bus or roaming around your house. There wouldn't have been anyone you were accountable to at those times. After school you might have romped about with your dog or gone off for a bike ride, or met some neighbourhood friends. After chowing down on a cheese sandwich you probably tried to avoid your homework by diving into a book or watching some TV. Other people would probably start to arrive home and you may have helped lay the table before everyone sat down to eat together. After that, homework would have been unavoidable.

So lucky you, you would have had some time when your head could be full of nothing more than empty air, some helping time, some social time, some family chat, and some study. Who would have cared how your hair looked? These days, unless you ban all devices for some hours after school and enforce everyone eating together, it won't be like this at all.

MENTAL STRESS

Teens – even when they are physically away from their friends, can feel either swamped or anxious that they need to keep in constant touch. Since they are much less likely to be allowed to roam around the neighbourhood, they do not have the outlet of physical exercise and they have almost no time when their minds aren't buzzing. Devices are built to fit right into people's comfort zones and so it's little wonder that the young ones in the family default to YouTube or gaming whenever possible: it's a clever combination of stimulation and soothing that we used to get from TV or magazines – but less efficiently. And of course, screens have a strong tendency to be addictive to younger minds. Therefore, screens fulfil multiple functions in a teen's life. They are the thing that they 'have to' have access to at all times; they are an important social platform but also a source of anxiety. At the same time, they contain addictive entertainment – and are thought to be the means of connection to the young person's most important group of people: their peers.

A PARALLEL UNIVERSE

You might remember that when you were in high school, adults seemed to have little to do with your world. They seemed fussy and had odd ways. They were preoccupied with things they keep hammering on about, which seemed to have little to do with what looked fun or important to you. Instead, life's zing came from getting together with friends. That's where dreams were aired and confidences exchanged. Daring plans were made – which got more daring, the more of you that got together. A large part of your life would have been focused on avoiding the whole world of adults' requirements while weirdly, you would have wanted to meekly comply with others. Sound familiar?

In some ways, teenagers believe that adults are just dumb and worry about dumb things. Grownups don't know how to have fun. Crucially, they don't share the rampaging hormones and the need for adrenaline that healthy young people experience. And along with that, please note that teenagers harbour a funny delusion. In amongst all of their irregular behaviours and their on–off sense of power, they are nearly oblivious to the fact that they are dependent upon adults for everything. They seem to have almost no realisation that someone else is paying all of the bills, cooking, keeping the house clean, and keeping a roof over their heads (remember this one, it will be important later). At this life stage, they are egocentric (i.e., preoccupied with themselves and their issues) and have a strong propensity to live in a fantasy world. When you realise this, it falls into place that their understanding about how a house works, let alone how the world really works, is very hazy indeed. This shines a light onto the fact that, as intelligent as they may be, their grasp of complex issues, relationships, events, and consequences is still developing. So, while we may urge our kids to 'study hard for their future' or 'not worry about what the others are posting about them', they are not yet able to see the whole landscape... the one that we find so important.

Adults think in very linear ways, such as:

STUDY HARD → GET A GOOD QUALIFICATION →

GET A GOOD JOB → EARN MONEY →

FEEL SECURE → HAVE A GOOD LIFE

Some of this is what we've learned through bitter experience. Teenagers, on the other hand, are gripped by the present moment and this is pretty unshakeable. Generally speaking, this is why schools have such a lot of rules and so many ways of urging students on (underpinned by well-known warnings and sanctions). If it were not so, schools would be very different places! Imagine – the teachers would be sitting in hubs ready to be used as consultants by eager and serious students who would be either planning out their next assignment or forming long queues for the library.

Altogether, teens are looking vulnerable when it comes to making decisions and managing the impacts of things in their world. And we haven't even mentioned something which has been increasing in its effect over the last century and which now seems to have got out of all control:

COMPARISON

If you watch a REALLY old movie (like, from the 1940s) from time to time you'll hear this phrase being mentioned:

"You have to know your place."

What a ghastly idea, and how unkind. It was designed to suppress people. But there is another meaning to it: that is that people should not wear themselves out dreaming of something that would just not be possible for them. The reality of the 1930s and 40s period was that social mobility was hardly happening. The mass media was pretty effective by then, but it was at arm's length. You would have had to buy a newspaper or go to the movies to get involved, and few magazines existed. You might have dreamed what it would be like to be a movie star but there was little sense that most people could actually be one. So, your life would have been based on the people and opportunities which were immediately around you. Common sense was a highly valued virtue – and dreaming big dreams was largely ridiculed.

People have always had the tendency to compare themselves to others but the opportunities for it then were much narrower. Gradually the triggers to us comparing ourselves with others have progressively increased through television in the 60s, the explosion of teen magazines in the 70s, pornography in the 80s – and mobile phones and the Internet from the 90s. And now its impact is massive.

It's lucky that now we have much more real social mobility. But somehow we are being led to believe that we could all be anything when actually, our talents may not lead us that way. Unfortunately, at some stage most teens will actually believe that they

- ❖ could/should be the world's top gamer
- ❖ could/should be a YouTube star
- ❖ could/should have a blog with a million followers
- ❖ could/should look exactly like the celebrity that their boyfriend/girlfriend spends so much time looking at on their screen
- ❖ Could/should drive a customised Jeep, wear lots of real gold bling and go on constant exotic holidays. Their parents must be stupid if they don't, or can't, provide it to their kids.

The anxiety which arrives when young people get flickers of realisation that this might not be possible, is anything but amusing.

UPWARD.... UPWARD... UPWARD...

The reason that kids constantly compare themselves to the beautiful and well-off people who are all over the media is that we humans all have a quirk. The majority of comparison that we engage in, is 'upward'. **We look *up* at people who might be our age but who are more successful/ well-off/glamorous/clever/beautiful than we are.** This vulnerability is in our DNA, and wall-to-wall media and our window into other people's lives is igniting it into a widespread wildfire.

Result: we feel inadequate and miserable by comparison. Rarely do we automatically look at people who are *worse* off than we are and think, 'Wow. I'm glad that's not me.'

The problem is that teens are no different: and with the devices they have access to which contain virtually endless examples of apparently fascinating and glamorous people who look so much better than they are, it becomes positively dangerous.

Many scientific studies have shown that in our complex world, we need fast-acting strategies which buffer us against upsetting events and threats to our self-esteem. For example, more robust people are known to access almost automatic processes which downgrade potentially demoralising feedback and re-adjust their self-view to re-set their feeling of wellbeing.[26]

> The letter says I didn't get into McSnooty College.
> Oh God. (pause) Well…
> *I wouldn't have liked it there, anyway.*
> *None of my friends will be going.*

> Sarah said she thought my passing in the game was
> rubbish. *Well – what does she know?*

Here are a couple of examples:

Interestingly enough, we all have a bit of an idea about this process and we also use it to help other people.

How often have you heard this one?

> No! He dumped you? What a ****. Listen.
> Seriously – he was never good enough for you,
> anyway. I never liked him.

As we get older and learn to manage living in a world which contains some pretty random events and lots of challenges, we need to buffer ourselves. So – we are supposed to evolve lots of our own strategies to:

* Help ourselves to feel **Special**
* **Deflect** some of the information which might make us feel downgraded
* Compare ourselves **Favourably** to others

❖ ...and help ourselves feel comfortable by rather **Over-Estimating** our part in positive events.

We need to learn to do this **just enough** to feel ok...and not so much that we turn onto raving narcissists.

If you think about it, most of us know this and we use it to help our children when they are small:

Ella, I know you didn't get an invitation to that party. But you *have* been invited to Georgie's and you like her much better, don't you?

Your picture didn't get a place in the Awards? Never mind. I like yours the best of all of them.

When we do this, we are not just trying to make our child feel better in the moment. We are also unconsciously trying to implant a script into their heads which they can carry along with them, and do it for themselves later. Just don't take it to ridiculous lengths, though – like this lady from way back in the 1940s:

Your Passing Out Parade was awesome, Johnny. You were the best. Everyone else was marching out of step except for you!

This sort of unreality produces pampered princes and princesses who have no realistic idea of their own capabilities.

But – back to the issue of Comparison. It is clear that these days, our teenagers are comparing themselves to far too many others (i.e., the pool is too big) and they are comparing themselves to people who are not really part of their world: they are part of the cyber-world. What chance do they have of feeling ok about themselves under these conditions? It is a worry.

So – what can we do to help?

> **Keep it local**
>
> **Keep it real**
>
> **Let them spend time with their talents**
>
> **Change the upward comparison**
>
> **Build positive, calm dialogue**

KEEP IT LOCAL

One antidote to this flood of unreality is to keep leading the child back to touchstones which are a part of real life, and which they can experience regularly. The task is – at each phase of their development – to establish reality 'Nodes' which they will get to know and accept, and which will provide a counterbalance to the idiocy which is out there – and which they find very hard to tell from reality.

7-year-old Elly says:

'Mum, I am going to be the Champion of Junior Masterchef. I will be famous and get on TV. I want to make cakes like that.'

(The 10-year-old contestant on the TV screen has just made a perfect three-layer caramel cake with elaborate spun- sugar decoration on top, with no adult help.)

Mum can say,
'I see. You like your cooking, don't you? Last week you almost made cupcakes by yourself. Let's decide what kind of ones you want to have a go at next. And – how about you practice your skills in making the icing look really nice?'

If Elly really does like cooking, her Mum could make this a regular activity. It would be very good for Elly to take some of her creations to large family or community events where they would be welcomed. At the same time, she could see for herself how her work stacks up. She will probably discover that yes – she is good at cooking – but that this whole area is much more tricky than it looks on TV and 'perfect' isn't at all easy.

KEEP IT REAL

The best reality-checkers are activities that end up being regular, and that the child is invested in. It is better still if a parent is also involved so that the two can have lots of conversations about the child's evolving goals: the child will quickly learn about their own capacities and limitations and will start to ask for help in trying to overcome these.

Child: 'Dad, I really lost it on that last obstacle. I just couldn't hold the bike up enough. I want to be like Jordan – he always wins.'

Dad: 'Jordan is a lot taller and bigger than you are. And he's older, so he has had time to build up more muscle to hold the bike through the big jumps. Don't forget he's had his own problems. Remember how he broke his collar bone in that fall last year?'

LET THEM SPEND TIME WITH THEIR TALENTS

Here is a child who is experienced in their hobby being asked about it by a family visitor:

Visitor: 'I was watching you do that round. How do you tell when to speed the horse up and when to steady him? And – were you telling him to lengthen his stride between those last two jumps?'

Jacinta: 'Umm – all horses are different and some just need to go faster. But Ned rushes mostly. In the first round you don't need so much speed – you just need a perfect round so you qualify. Speed is for the second round. Ned likes that! Yep, you do need to get the strides right. So, we get to walk the course before we ride it and because we know how long our own horse's stride is, we have to calculate. That bit actually does my brain in!'

Visitor: 'I think you did a great job. You obviously know what you are doing.'

As you can see, when the child is able to build up technical skills, this is a great asset. It helps them to feel competent, while at the same time providing them with a very clear appreciation of how complex things are, and what they can and cannot do just yet. For a child, that is a great method to help them appraise reality.

CHANGE THE UPWARD COMPARISON

Have a look at this diagram. Here is a person – maybe located about two-thirds of the way up the pyramid in the field they are most interested in (it could be general academic ability, basketball or hockey skills, dancing/anything).

But how might they compare themselves? Most likely not to all of the people who are below them. Instead, they may do what we are all constantly encouraged to do – to look UPWARDS and compare themselves not only to the handful of people in the world who are at the pinnacle of the pyramid. That is amply illustrated by the old quip which says that there are *7.5 billion people in the world.... but only 8 working Supermodels.* How's that for a ludicrous basis for comparison? Additionally, this person is comparing themselves on multiple skills dimensions.

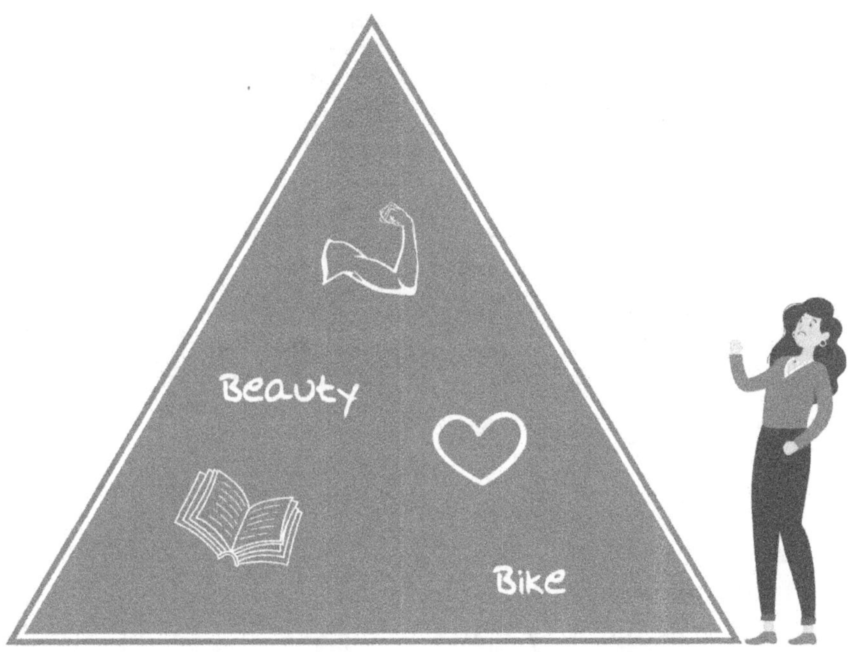

Since most of us are wired-up to make upward comparisons, here is how we can alter the process so it is less harmful.

Here, the little person looking at the pyramid, is comparing themselves on only ONE dimension - the one they are most interested in (e.g., cycling). And instead of trying to be Marianne Vos, they can look in detail at the skills of someone they can actually see and know. In this way, they can use the more local person's achievements to motivate and encourage themselves – while not feeling nearly as intimidated. It's a bit like having a mentor-figure to look up to and be inspired by. ***Reachability is the key.***

BUILD POSITIVE CALM DIALOGUE

The 'Nodes' described in the Keep it Local section above, can really assist a child to appreciate the grittiness and imperfection of reality – in one sphere. But youngsters are still vulnerable to spinning out and losing their judgement with the sheer range of things which pass in and out of their field of interest. We've all had crazes on something which our neighbour or best friend does. It seems urgent and all-involving at the time, but it often turns out to be just plain inappropriate. The level of drama along the way shows how intense the child or teenager's emotions are at the time.

Sindra: 'Makeup is my life, Mum. I want to have an amazing makeup blog like that Kassy girl. She makes thousands of dollars! Why won't you let me get my eyebrows tinted and my eyelashes extended? Why won't you let me post the best pictures of me up so people can see? I need this, you're ruining my life and you're not letting me practice the thing I love best.'

Mum: 'That Kassy girl is aged about 22 darling. We are just not allowed to do those things when we are 14. We actually would not know who was looking at you on the Net and we need to be safe. How about we build up your skills so that by the time you are older they will be amazing? How about we make you the go-to girl for your friends' makeup? You could invite them around before parties and you could do it for them. If you want to extend your skills you could maybe practice doing the makeup for the next school production. Shall we make a list of the materials you need and we can save up to buy it bit by bit?'

Here's Sindra, aged 14:

This mum has spotted that Sindra is comparing herself (impossibly) to someone who is older and who lives in a different world. Wisely, she has re-focused her daughter's attention on what is local, achievable, and safe – but which still allows challenge and growth.

LOOKS

For girls especially, this form of comparison has become potentially distressing and almost endless in its scope. Lovely girls at their fleeting best are paraded on TV, in music videos, adverts, and plastered wall-to-wall all over the internet. For vulnerable and developing young girls who anxiously browse for hours, comparing themselves unfavourably to each model they see, this spells misery. It drives down their sense of value in the world. What can we do?

Unfortunately, the remedy for this takes a very long time. The girl will need her attention re-focused on two things at intervals until her sense of herself has finally become stronger than the barrage of external images. The two things are:

1. Positive but realistic self-acceptance
2. Well-rounded self-valuing

POSITIVE BUT REALISTIC SELF-ACCEPTANCE

Here is a mum tackling the first part with her 12-year-old daughter:

'I know what you mean, honey. That girl's nose doesn't look like yours. But have a look at mine. It doesn't, either! I have learned to like this nose. That's because it is part of me. All of me is me! And no-one else can ever be like me. Haha. I am a walking talking me and here I am. I look like my aunty Lessa and I don't want anyone to take that away.

By the way, I like my arms and legs, too. We wouldn't want to change those, would we?'

This kind of message might need to be repeated many times over the years until the little girl has successfully built her own solid confidence. Watch out for the girl who spent a period of time talking about this topic but then goes quiet for some time – but looks haunted. What may she be thinking inside?

There are many different types of exercise to assist with the Looks issue. Here is one we can do with the 12-year-old girl to assist with:

Ok. Look at all of you. Now tell me - which one of your friends should change the way she looks?'

Child: 'Whaat?'

Mum: 'Thought so. Now let's look at each of your friends in turn. I want you to tell me what each one of them means to you. I want you to tell me why you love how each one of your friends' looks. Then I want you to tell me exactly what you like about each friend.'

(After the exercise)

Mum: 'Good. Well done! So you see, pumpkin, how you look is just a representation of who you are. It is so we can recognise you. It is not the whole of who you are. You can only really know the people whom you are close to and whom you love. Then you know what they really are and why you love them as you do. We all need to be ourselves. And it is lovely.'

Well-rounded self-valuing

Well-rounded self-valuing continues to build as we mature. We all need the opportunity to realise what we are good at and why we like our own values and goals. We build up faith in ourselves, bit by bit.

CHAPTER 8

HOW TEENAGERS ARE WIRED

Teenage neurological and emotional development

Like it or not, we humans are very complex beings. As such, we take a very long time to grow to maturity – and need a lot of help along the way. A 16-year-old, for example, is very different to a 24-year-old. A quick check on their physical appearance will tell us that, and the still-developing factor is also evident in the brain.

The teenage years feature very rapid developments in the brain. These mean that cognitively, teenagers are becoming much more able. And they soon become very aware of this. With a faster processing speed and improved 'distributed processing', they are able to reach into all sorts of new possibilities ('distributed processing' refers to the brain's ability to co-ordinate activities across its different areas). What teens are less aware of, is that their capacity for reasoning all the way to a conclusion is still relatively poor. Additionally, their ability to engage in interactive debate in a way that we would consider thoughtful is just beginning. If you are not sure about this, think back to a time when you tried to have a reasoned debate with a young teen who felt passionately about something. They may not always be able to validate your point of view and often find it hard to develop new directions in a debate.

Here's an example:

Uncle: 'Mum says you've had a note back about needing to get your hair cut for school. And there's some stuff about your uniform as well?'

Al: 'It's all rubbish. I should be able to have long hair and not wash it if I want to. And uniform is just control by the system.'

Uncle: 'But you like your school – and the uniform and hair stuff is part of their rules.'

Al: 'But it shouldn't apply to me.'

Uncle: 'Well, you could always go to our local school – their rules are more relaxed.'

Al: 'But I have a scholarship.'

Uncle: 'Maybe your school feels it has to present itself a certain way because it charges fees.'

Al: 'That's nothing to do with me.'

This combination of faster thinking and more access to ideas coupled with lower reasoning power can mean lots of arguments!

SOCIAL DEVELOPMENT

As they become less physically dependent upon their sheltering family, the teenager finds their peer networks *very* important. The desire for independence is an essential part of growing up – or we would all still be sitting in our parents' kitchens. However, starting to peel away from parents and siblings as the main emotional supports and turning to friends instead, brings a feeling of urgency about feeling accepted. Only a true 'loner' feels relatively immune from all the varieties of peer pressure: not many teenagers would identify themselves in this way. This often means that teenagers feel they have to match their group in their style of dress, the way they speak, their food preferences, which bands they like... and what they find wrong with the world of adults.

Several researchers have pointed to people in their teenaged years being more strongly connected to rewards.[27,28] This is thought to be related to developments in the dopamine-regulated systems within the brain. Dopamine is a substance which is key to our sensitivity towards rewards and to the development of addictive behaviours.[29] For the teenager, this may mean that they are more highly motivated by all kinds of potential rewards from peer acceptance, to foods, to gaming.

SHAPING

The adolescent development period in the brain features massive re-organisations, with some types of operations fading in importance while others gain ground. In this way, the *types* of experiences and learning the teenager is exposed to can be critical in shaping their development.

For example, if the teen experiences a lot of family discussion and debate, they will learn great strengths in this area over time. But if they are taught to fight, argue, and respond aggressively then these responses will become very dominant. To some extent the learned pathways become wired-in. So it is crucial that during this period of development the person is given repeated experiences which are helpful and which guide their haphazardly growing skills.

INHIBITORY MECHANISMS

As the taste for rewards is growing and the desire to belong and feel accepted by peers is taking centre stage, one other factor in the adolescent brain is also important. What we call 'inhibitory mechanisms' are still very much under construction – and in the early- to mid-teenage years, these are largely outpaced by the rapid increase in overall brain size. Inhibitory mechanisms include activities that are like the 'police officers' of the brain and reside in the pre-frontal cortex. These are the processes which lead us to exercise judgement and caution. For example, if your child wants to join a group of friends who – in an adrenaline rush – are planning to rampage around jumping on the bonnets of cars, you would hope that these cautionary processes would send messages such as 'don't think I want to be caught doing that', or 'what might happen if I go along with that?' But in adolescents, these processes are still under-developed and are often overwhelmed by the rush they experience from thrill-seeking and taking part in something with their peers, which brings the sense of belonging. For this reason, it is very important not just to tell your child off but to get them to work through the possible consequences of different scenarios *themselves* so that they learn something. Just another 'adult lecture' will not teach their brains anything very much.

EMOTION-REGULATION

Teenagers are renowned for their mercurial emotions. Argumentative one moment and mopey the next, exasperated parents are often tempted to respond as if these sudden changes are deliberate (or just self-indulgent). Teenagers do admittedly experience a great deal of self-focus. That is, their view of themselves is immature. Rather than seeing themselves as having a place in the landscape, which includes other people who have needs, concerns, and constrains, their own preoccupations loom very large and blot out much of what is around them. This tends to explain actions such as taking the rest of the milk and not leaving any for anyone else; leaving their rubbish everywhere; not taking part in chores (which then has an impact on others) … the list goes on and on.

It is not yet really known whether taking the whole perspective develops automatically on its own with age, or whether it needs a booster with lots of teaching. Most likely, this is dependent upon the person's temperament to an extent – that is, a thoughtful and sensitive individual will be more likely to join these dots themselves while a bullish and less mature person will not. Either way, it's interesting. I'd be willing to bet that you have had conversations like this one in your houschold:

Mum: 'Olly, you should have taken the bus home.'

Olly: 'Why? Dad can always give me a lift. I'd only been a couple of hours at the mall after school and the buses get less at that time.'

Mum: 'You know, though, that Dad works late on a Thursday so he's tired. Plus, he stops on the way home to get us takeaway as I'm at Athletics with Cooper. So, if he has to go out of his way, not only is he tired, but we all eat late.'

Olly: ,Ohhhhh…'

Often, if we can outline the different considerations in a situation (without the teenager getting mad) this will connect the dots for them, and they will learn something. If you have brought up older teenagers already, you might feel that it takes a couple of years of examples like this – along with the natural maturational process – for the young person to do this on their own behalf and without any prompting.

With all of the competing priorities and physical shifts that are going on, accompanied by a relatively immature brain, it is little wonder that teenaged people often find it hard to regulate their emotions. They may quickly feel overwhelmed by anger or sadness, or feelings of injustice – and they may have few strategies which they are used to using. One of the problems is that:

a) they probably feel like a completely different person to the one they were last year, and so

b) they have had little practice in how to manage all of this within themselves.

Adults don't have these excuses! We have had years to get used to how our particular emotions react and we have a great deal at our disposal which assists us. Don't think so? Well – we usually have car keys, another adult to speak to, access via vehicle to a doctor or pharmacy for remedies, some cash to pay for these, access to health systems and their advice and knowledge, hopefully access to our own front door and some degree of control over our home environment. A teenager has precisely none of the above.

HORMONES

Whole books could (and have) been written about the physiology and impacts of fast-developing hormonal changes for the young human. So, I'll be brief. We are all probably vaguely familiar with the notion that the increase in (predominantly) testosterone in boys, and (predominantly) oestrogen and progesterone in girls has impacts that we roll our eyes over in adult company. We expect that a boy might get more aggressive, more sweaty and smelly for a while, and more prone to strong sexual interests as he develops. And we might predict that a girl would get more moody and/or teary as puberty takes over. But other things are going on in their biochemistry as well. Not only is more adrenaline produced in the teenaged body,[30] but this can become an upwards spiral as a teenager's craving for rewards, thrill-feelings and their desire to keep up with their friends, become more evident. Yet, because teenagers are highly prone to stress, the fallout from a lot of adrenaline in the bloodstream is that extra cortisol (the so-called 'stress hormone') goes up exponentially. This means that they are likely to experience a cascade of biochemical factors from within which lead to increased agitation at the same time as they are feeling increased pressures from their new values and from their peer group.

Let's summarise the factors we've identified so far:

Cognitive Factors
- ❖ Increasing processing speed in the brain
- ❖ Increasing general cognitive capacity
- ❖ Greater imaginative power
- ❖ Relatively poor ability in reasoned argument
- ❖ High degree of self-focus
- ❖ Poorer capacity for perspective-taking
- ❖ Highly driven by rewards
- ❖ Highly driven by the pleasure of 'thrill'
- ❖ Low level of inhibitory mechanisms
- ❖ Poorer ability to see the chain of consequences

Social factors
- ❖ Greater desire for independence
- ❖ Less attention to parents as a credible source
- ❖ Urgent desire to be with peers
- ❖ Urgent desire to be fully accepted by peers
- ❖ Fear of rejection by peers

Hormonal Influences
- ❖ Possible increase in moodiness/tearfulness
- ❖ Increase in sexual interests

* More adrenaline
* Higher stress, but poor stress tolerance
* Higher levels of cortisol

If you add all of these together, it begins to look like a complex mixture. Don't forget that the teenager is also dealing with these as well:

* Family expectations – which often get repeated over and over
* Family clashes over school progress and behaviour
* Stresses associated with the academic part of school: achievement level, homework load, possibly feeling not 'good enough' in some subjects
* Skin breakouts, fat deposits appearing where they never have before; perceived faults in one's physique – just when peer approval feels most critical
* Social media – and all it brings with it
* The start of romantic relationships
* Questions about our personality and identity

Given all of this, it is little wonder that those 'teenage volcanoes' can be heard popping and crackling in most homes across the land. Perhaps for once we should be glad that we are adults!

HINTS TO HELP...

❖ Remember that teenagers are smart – but should not be expected to use reasoning, empathy, and self-pacing in an argument like you can. Just stay mellow on your own part!

❖ Remember that peers seem all-important at this age... and don't worry too much about the apparent rebellion and the over-valuing of other teens' ideas that comes with this. It is your job to stay in the background, and help to guide them through.

❖ Remember that teenagers' behaviours will sometimes be distorted by peer pressure. Do not worry too much about this unless they become unresponsive to you or to the normal systems of law and the governance of empathy (which acts to slow down a lot of unwise actions).

❖ Remember that your teenager will often be reward-driven and have shifting emotions – cue the typical teenage behaviours!

❖ When they forget to place others' needs into the equation, join the dots for them in a way that does not insult them.

❖ When evidence of the 'hideous hormones' is apparent, remember how it was for you at their age… and that they are likely to have high levels of accompanying stress.

❖ Remember that underneath the apparent bravado, people in their teens are often highly confused and feel disempowered underneath it all. Uncertain about who they are and where they are going, they have a great deal to learn about how the world out there really works.

CHAPTER 9

OUR INFLUENCE

PARENTING BEHAVIOURS

In contemporary life we tend to make four basic errors when it comes to parenting decisions. The first is reacting out of time pressure. The second is acting from a basis of anxiety. The third is soft-pedalling. And the fourth is over-reacting. Our responses are unplanned, and we lack vision about how we want to shape our teens' development. We respond in the moment, but we don't really have a plan about what we are doing. We also tend to worry that others may disapprove of how we discipline our children; we may not be *following the pack*. As we rush about our lives, we often feel isolated when faced with quite powerful teenaged bad behaviours. And we don't always feel that we have backup from a cohesive culture that either supports us or provides guidelines for what we should do.

In prior times in the Western world, the guidance was simple: young people ought to do as they were told and behave. If they transgressed, the punishments were likely to be swift and maybe physical. Parental authority was everything and it was the young person who was isolated. As a consequence, things looked calm and predictable on the surface as everyone proceeded along conventional and well-ordered lines. At the same time, there are hundreds of stories of young people fleeing from their homes every year due to over-restriction and harsh punishments.

So, what can we do? It's all very well to try and operate via one of the parenting manuals. But when we are pressed for time, facing multiple demands from family members while trying to pick up one child from sports, calm down another and simultaneously planning dinner – what is really possible?

New behaviours in our kids often take us by surprise, and we don't know how to respond. It pays to be aware of what they can come up with, what the behaviours mean, and how we can safely intervene. Just to cheer you up, here's a great big list of some of the things we commonly get wrong. All of these will have a negative impact on teenagers who are becoming volatile.

Helicoptering

Alyssa (13): 'I'm not going to school. Jen said that she's not really my friend anymore. And the others in her group said they agreed. So now I've got no-one to hang out with. I can't go in because what about lunchtimes? I'm so angry, it's not fair.'

Mum: 'That is bullying. Don't worry, darling, I will go in and talk to Mrs McKenzie. Those girls are not to exclude you. And I will catch up with Jen's mum at my Netball group and I'll tell her what's what.'

We need to be careful about behaviours from peers. There is a big range, from normal 'kid' thoughtlessness and rudeness to teasing and then on to organised victimisation and exclusion (which can truly be called bullying). This example looks like normal friendship movements (teenage girls have notoriously volatile friendship patterns). What this mum is doing will disempower Alyssa from being able to negotiate the normal – if painful – parts of peer relationships. Jen probably hasn't done anything wrong – and what Alyssa needs is confidence and skills. It is unlikely to be the last time she experiences issues like this in her high school career.

Hectoring

Steve and Hartley (13 & 14) were at their baseball club. Instead of staying around and watching as they were supposed to, they went behind the line of trees and into bushland. Not only are there snakes by the creek, but there have been incidents of indecent exposure towards children recently – and no-one has yet been apprehended.

Dad: 'What the hell are you doing here? How many times have I told you that you're not to come out here without an adult? You are both so disobedient. Look at the other kids – they are all doing what they are supposed to. It's just you two misbehaving AGAIN. I'm so fed up with it and I am ashamed of you. You make me look stupid to the other parents. You are coming back with me.'

This is a good one. Here's something important to remember: adults *love* to talk and talk at their kids. But kids don't work like that. Not only is it offensive, it quickly becomes ineffective. We will re-visit this quite a few times – but if you need to talk to your kids 'in the moment' or 'on the spot', keep it *very, very brief.* And try not to lose your temper. Remember, kids are wired to try silly things and to crave adventures. I'd be very scared if they *didn't.* Stepford Wives, anyone? It's our job to try our best to keep a lookout and save them from some of the perils that are out there.

Here's what the dad could have done:

Keep it Brief

Dad: 'Here you are. Guys, you know you're not supposed to be out here and you know why. We'll talk about it later. Back into the clubhouse. Now.'

Allowing Escalation

Mum has discovered Shiv (15) to be still on his laptop an hour after he is supposed to stop…

Mum: 'It is one hour since you are supposed to have put this away! I can't believe you did that, put it away now. I'm taking it off you tomorrow – there'll be no screen time at all for two days.'

Shiv: 'It's your fault I did that – you didn't tell me what the time was. I need reminding. I was only chatting with friends. And you're so unfair, you're such a harpy – none of my mates' mums lay down the law like you do. They are all reasonable parents. Not like you.'

Mum: 'A harpy! How dare you! I've been on the phone organising your soccer practice at BOTH of your clubs for the next school term. You are so ungrateful. I am angry with you. You have a rude attitude and I can't stand it. You are just like your father. Ungrateful and rude.'

Well, this exchange isn't going to a good place…

We'll talk much more about responses to thoughtless and boundary-breaking teens later on, but in this case, four mistakes are being made:

1. Teens get rude. It's a fact of life and it's not a disaster. It's usually best not to respond to it on the spot as this is fraught with perils. Keep your adult power up your sleeve and attend to it later…
2. Mum has lost her temper. Always a mistake with teens – this leads to the 'Fire' that we don't want to see….
3. Mum has facilitated an escalation when it is her job to keep some reasonable authority in the situation. She has lost her adult position here.
4. Mum has issued some nasty insults. Shiv will be oblivious to the ones he has uttered, but he will remember these from Mum…

Allowing a Lengthy Exchange

This one is a bit similar…

Stepdad: 'Did you take that lasagne out of the fridge? That was for Anna when she gets home. We've told you that things in the microwaveable containers are for someone's dinner and they are not to be taken.'

Jason (16): 'There's not enough stuff here that I like. I'm always hungry around now, it's too long until dinner. Why shouldn't I take it? She probably won't be back, anyway, she'll be out with her friends. You don't leave enough stuff out for us.'

Stepdad: 'What? Don't be daft, there's heaps in the cupboard. You just need to have a look.'

Jason: 'Why should I? I'm too busy, I've got homework to do. You and Mum aren't doing a very good job.'
Stepdad: '*!x##^!'

Teens seem tricky to us and they can be mouthy at the drop of a hat. Why encourage it? It leads nowhere fast, an argument develops, and no-one wins. If your family are aware of the rules then the exchange can be simpler and it can stay civil:

> **State the Rules**
>
> Stepdad: 'You know the rules, buddy. Stuff in the microwaveable containers is someone's dinner. Suggest you get thinking of something to cook to replace it…'
>
> Jason: 'What!?'
>
> Stepdad: 'Get thinking then.' (Leaves)

> **GOLDEN RULE #1**
>
> State a rule simply, suggest a solution
> **AND THEN LEAVE**

This is solid gold. It is likely to remain respectful on your part; it retains your authority (but not in an offensive way), it takes the wind out of their sails, and it avoids the build-up of a nasty exchange that then affects everyone uncomfortably. Remember – YOU are the manager of these situations.

NEWSFLASH!

Teens behave badly. We are meant to be the ones who can de-escalate the situation so everyone can move on.

Here are some more...

Appeasing

Amy (15): 'Why did you get this horrible blue costume? How can I ever use this? It's rubbish.'

Mum: 'I thought the blue was nice. Won't it look good against what the other girls are wearing?'

Amy: 'Seriously, Mum, what did I just tell you? It's bloody rubbish, I can't.'

Mum: 'Oh, honey, don't feel bad. I'll go to the outfitters tomorrow and get something different, I'll just have to leave work early, though...'

What?

This mum is teaching her daughter that:

1. It's ok to be rude to your family.
2. If you yell 'jump' your mother will ask 'how high?'
3. Empathy for others is not taught in this family.
4. Mum is teaching Amy that she does not have to try and keep her temper; does not have to care for Mum's feelings; does not have to take part in solving any problems herself; does not have to show respect; and that belligerence wins.

P.S. Mum is to be treated as a doormat.

Following

Mum: 'Jordan, are you ready to take Maya to her practice? It'll only take you 10 minutes to walk there.'

Jordan (17): 'Nah. Not doing it. Told you I hate it there. I'm meeting the guys at the mall and we're going to a movie.'

Mum: 'What? You're not serious. This means a lot to Maya and I have to go and pick up my test results. Please get ready and take her.'

Jordan: 'Nah.' (Walks away to his room.)

Mum – following: 'Come back here! This is important. Don't go into your room – get out here now.' (Tries to push his door open).

Jordan (Puts his foot against the door): 'Piss off! I told you I'm busy! Cow. Leave me alone.'

Mum: 'Open this door! This is my house! Who do you think puts a roof over your head?'Jordan: (Shouting unrepeatable expletives…)

This scenario might look appalling, but it is all too common. Any 17-year-old is occasionally capable of behaviour like this but if he has not been given regular chores, does not take part in teamwork activities with his mother, and has not successfully been given boundaries up to now, this will make such reactions much more likely. This young man is showing a risky level of poor empathy to his family as well as rudeness and contempt. His mother is right – where does he most likely get the money to go to the movies?

What could Mum have done instead?

> **Deal with it later**
>
> Mum: (Peels off and walks away…)

Following teens acts as an escalation and as soon as you follow – they feel in control of the situation. But it never goes anywhere good: witness the foot in the door and the toxic yelling and verbal attack.

Instead, Mum can take Maya with her to the doctor's office or drop her on the way and then go back.

Mum now has at her disposal the means to deal with Jordan later – at any time of her choosing.

Now who is feeling stronger?

Punishing/Grounding/Banning

Dad: 'Now that's done it. This is an email from the school saying that you haven't handed in your final English assignment at all. You lied to me, Ken. And I know why you didn't do it – it'll be because you were up all night playing games online. Well – your iPad is gone for a month/OR – you are grounded for a month/OR – you are banned from all basketball matches for a month.'

> Ken (16): 'Whaaat? I hate you. You don't care about me at all. No-one else's parents act this way. You are wrecking my life.'

Punishing, grounding, and banning. Parents most likely feel that they have to do *something*. And they should take away *something*. The most obvious thing to remove is a sport or electronic devices – and the angrier we feel, the longer we take them away for!

So – what's wrong with that?

Here is what's wrong with that:

1. It is usually a knee-jerk reaction. With teens you don't have to react in the moment (i.e., just to have something to say)
2. If you give a consequence in a state of anger, it's hardly going to be the best-designed move you've ever made, is it?
3. You're escalating again
4. Giving long bans or withdrawals of objects wears down after a few days. The teen sulks but kind of gets used to it. And the adult <u>has already run out of any other consequences for the rest of the month.</u> Horrors!

Now again, the following suggestions will only really work if you have (or are working to) establish some basic trust with your child, and if you have (or are working to) establish non-volatile ways to discipline.

What could Dad have done?

Respond with Calm

Dad (has waited till he feels sane): 'Ken – this email says that you haven't submitted your final English task at all.'

Ken: 'Whaat? Oh. Yeh. Unhh. Shit. I just couldn't do it, Dad. It didn't make any sense at all. Plus umm, I was online a lot around then. There was all that trouble around Jackson doing online bullying, remember?'

Dad: 'What do you think is going to happen since you haven't done the task? This looks like a fail for the year.'

Ken: 'No. What? Hell. What can we do, Dad?'

Dad: 'I will call your Year Co-ordinator and ask for some special consideration due to the Jackson stuff, which did upset everyone. BUT – you will have to talk to her, too, and admit your part in not doing the assignment. This is a last-chance thing, buddy – there's no way they'd give you any leeway a second time.'

Ken: 'Ok, Dad. Phew. Sorry.'

As you can see above, Dad on his second go achieves a great dialogue. His son is not defensive and Dad can use his wisdom about how he can approach the issue to the best effect. Good outcome, Dad.

Here are another Two Golden Rules with teens:

> ### GOLDEN RULE #2
>
> Do not say anything when you feel negative emotions

Teens have a unique piece of equipment that they carry around with them everywhere. It is **a Big Red Button** and it is connected directly to adults' emotions (especially their parents'). At the drop of a hat, they press it and *Hey, Presto!* Parents are upset and feel like they don't know what to do (but they feel they have to do *something* – usually yell). As we've seen, this never takes things to a good place.

> ### GOLDEN RULE #3
>
> Either wait till you are calm – or act as if you are completely calm… before sailing through your house…

Once you have grasped some of these techniques and you feel you can use them – you will feel a lot calmer. Once you feel calm about responding to your teenagers, you can also feel some things you may not have felt for a while:

Creative – when you realise that you have lots of choices in how you respond to your teenager, you'll feel creative again.

Free – when you have experienced some success with your responses you will stop feeling like you are painted in a corner every time there is conflict or your teenager is rude.

A Fun Person – when you feel free and creative – you'll get your sense of humour back – which gives you licence to be your original kooky self! (i.e., no longer a grumpy, worn-out person who never feels loved and who never feels off-duty).

But – how do we do this? What are these techniques that will give us back our sanity?

See the next chapter…

REMINDERS

Try and remember not to get involved with the following:

- ❖ Helicoptering
- ❖ Hectoring
- ❖ Allowing escalation
- ❖ Allowing a lengthy exchange
- ❖ Appeasing
- ❖ Following
- ❖ … and limit the Punishing/Grounding/Banning

And remember our Golden Rules 1-3:

Golden Rule #1

State a rule simply, suggest a solution, AND THEN LEAVE.

Golden Rule #2:

Do not say anything when you feel negative emotions.

Golden Rule #3:

Either wait till you are calm – or act as if you are completely calm… before sailing through your house….

CHAPTER 10

THE BAD BEHAVIOURS – AND HOW TO RESPOND TO THEM

TYPES OF BEHAVIOURS

Have teenagers all been to the same secret college or something? If you talk to your friends, you'll find that when teens are not being their best selves:

- ❖ They come up with the same types of behaviour
- ❖ They do this upon common triggers
- ❖ They even say some of the same things!

Why is this? Many of the answers lie in the issues we have discussed in previous chapters. That is, in our current society's complex climate, teenagers are at risk of becoming hostile, non-empathetic, avoidant, self-centred, over-entitled, unwilling, rude, verbally aggressive, and living in a fantasy land at times – if their development is not supported by the key strengthening factors that we can provide. Having said that, the triggers to these negative tendencies are many and they are all around every young person. The 'strengtheners' *reduce* these problems, but they can't eradicate them.

So what behaviours are we looking at?

Parents most commonly describe these behaviours when talking about teenaged actions that they find hard to manage:

- ❖ Rudeness
- ❖ Laziness
- ❖ Failure to co-operate
- ❖ Failure to do agreed chores
- ❖ Failure to do schoolwork
- ❖ Disrespect towards parents (often followed by walking out or walking away)
- ❖ Contempt
- ❖ Verbal aggression or verbal attack/being scathing
- ❖ Boundary-breaking
- ❖ Lying
- ❖ Threats
- ❖ Arguing back
- ❖ Escalating situations very quickly
- ❖ Minor stealing
- ❖ Disrespect or lack of co-operation with their siblings
- ❖ Constant negativity towards a stepparent[*]

DAMAGE

One of the biggest problems with these kinds of teenaged behaviours is that the kids themselves have no real perception of the damage they are doing to their relationship

---

[*] This last one reveals a complex situation and it needs an in-depth approach; similarly, substance abuse, running away, sexual violence, or promiscuity, significant threats to harm others or self and physical violence or property damage – need IMMEDIATE professional assistance for your family.

with their parents and possibly with the rest of the family. To have someone in your home respond unpredictably and with rudeness, contempt and power-seeking behaviours over some period of time can feel devastating. Mothers, especially, often describe that they feel 'destroyed' by the aggression and contempt from their offspring. They feel their affection and motivation ebbing away. As we said in the introduction, it seems a far cry from those early years when your small children showed you so much unconditional love.

But remember these key things:

1. In our culture, these behaviours are in the normal range for teenagers (unfortunately).

2. If you operate the techniques described to help your child along their development track, manage themselves independently, stay in step with the real world, and find agency and confidence, you'll have laid good groundwork.

3. Cool parental response techniques can make a real difference.

These aim to:

❖ Minimise (and even reverse) the damage
❖ Help the teen to travel on a much better track
❖ Help you to feel that you have your parental authority back once more
❖ Feel relaxed in your own home
❖ Help you feel like yourself again
❖ Help you feel 'I've got this'

How to begin?

> ## GOLDEN RULE #4
>
> Remember that these types of behaviour are happening in hundreds of houses in your suburb! They are not an emergency and you have got this. Therefore:
>
> ## DO NOT FEEL HURT

Put it this way: You wouldn't feel emotionally hurt if your 18-month-old came up and took a swipe at you, or if your three-year-old said, 'I wanted the ice cream! I hate you, Mummy/Daddy!' Do not take these behaviours to heart when they occur. *It is essential that you remain calm and in emotional 'neutral'* when you respond to these behaviours, which are the less-nice parts of a developmental phase.

Why? Because that is what will begin to save the day.

I spent some time working in a youth jail. It was fascinating, and it taught me a lot. At this venue, the officers were highly trained and well supported. They felt like they had the answers to most of the problems that arose. And they worked in small units that each had only a small number of young people and a high staff-to-inmate ratio. In a situation like this, it is easy to see that calmness and an unemotional response are what work best and not only that, they are absolutely necessary. Here is a typical scenario that we would see:

Manny is a 16-year-old youth recently arrived to the unit.
'I'm not doing that stuff, you can't make me.' He lashes out to try and take an object from the officer.

Officer no.1 steps closer to him and says: 'We don't do that here, buddy. We are all just about to have afternoon tea. Today, Jim and Trev have made chocolate carrot cake. But if you get physical, you'll have to go into the Quiet Room for a while, and you'll miss out. What's it to be?'

Manny lashes out again. Officer 1 and Officer 2 take a hold of him and without fuss, put him into the Quiet Room, which is a locked space. Through the large window, Manny can see that the two officers and the six other boys are making coffee and sitting down to eat the cake. They are all chatting about a football game whose result was hotly disputed!

Manny felt that he had an image to establish on his arrival at the unit. But he's seen how things work and tomorrow he's not going to want to miss out again.

You can see right away that the adults becoming emotional just wouldn't work. I've provided a polite example, and those officers would also have been on the receiving end of some eye-watering insults at times, and also physical attacks. But of course, they never retaliated, and they didn't take it personally.

You too, can be a professional. The officers had each other and they had great training. You may need to use the support of your partner or some strong self-talk to deal with the hurt feelings that arise from episodes of 'teen behaviour'. *But you need to do it.* Otherwise, you'll be responding from a highly emotional place – and a rather disabled one.

Let's tackle Rudeness right away.

STEP 1: RULES

> ### RULES FOR RUDENESS
>
> The first thing to do is to explain the rules for your house to your child at a 'neutral' time – i.e., when there is no arguing going on.

It might go like this:

> 'Jamie, I want to be clearer about what the rules are at home. That is: in our house we don't yell at each other; we don't use insults, we don't disrespect or use put-downs. Just so you know, there will be consequences if that does happen.'

Don't expect much of a reaction. But when your teen does break a rule, you can go to step 2.

STEP 2: RESPONDING

Here are 3 important methods for responding to your youths' bad behaviours: they are the first of our **Behaviour Support Principles.**

> ### BEHAVIOUR SUPPORT PRINCIPLES
>
> 1. You don't have to respond in the moment. You can wait for hours and sometimes days.
> 2. You don't have to provide a consistent (i.e., predictable) response.
> 3. You must be fair at all times.

What might this look like?

> Mum: 'Ally, that's the second time I've asked you to empty the dishwasher. It's your day today and it's on the roster. I first asked you 30 minutes ago.'
>
> Ally (15): 'I've told you, I'm busy. I'll do it later.'
>
> Mum: 'You did agree to that job, though: and we won't be able to put the dinner dishes in when it hasn't been unloaded. It'll impact on other people.'
>
> Ally: 'God, you're such a nag. Don't you ever shut up? Why don't you do it – you're only standing around, anyway. As usual. Duh.'
>
> (Stomps off to her room).

Mum now has choices.

Of course, she is **not** going to argue back, or follow Ally – which would be escalating the situation. She needs to take a deep breath and remind herself that this is a fine example of silly behaviours that are not hard to handle. Then, she waits.

What is she waiting for?

Mum is waiting for the opportunity that will inevitably come up – where it is the right time to address what Ally has done. It will probably be within the next few hours – or it might be the next day.

Here's a funny thing. Teens who are rude, offensive, refuse tasks, etc. – are built like boomerangs. Within hours – they are almost bound to come and ask/demand something from you.

Those times can be a great time to respond. This is where your power to discipline really lies. You should never be vindictive, flippant, or 'smart' – but what you can do is reflect what would happen in any other real relationship. That is, with respectfulness. Get your teenager to live in the real world.

It might look like this:

Ally - comes back into the kitchen 2 hours later. "Hey Muumm," (Wheedling). "It's Amy's birthday and we're all giving her gifts. I'd forgotten. Can I have $20 and can you take me to the mall? I need to get her something. Pleeease?"

Mum stays calm and keeps to her agenda. She speaks what feels *true* to her:

'Ally – you were really rude to me earlier. Not just that – pretty disrespectful, too. That is hurtful, you know? So, no. I won't be taking you. Sorry. Another time."

Ally: 'Whaat?!!' (Gasps).

This type of response is absolutely the right thing to do. Clear, respectful, and real – it is what Ally would receive (if she were lucky) from a future flatmate, partner, or best friend. It signals that she needs to attend to the relationship between her and her mum – not just use it as a football.

What most parents might have done in this situation is:

1. Followed/yelled/tried to shout it out through a locked door – but then most likely…
2. Given in to the later demand – albeit with some sulking, or a giant lecture.

What kind of relationship teaching is that?

A better response style gives you time to recover from your feelings and lets you wait until the correct time presents itself. Then you briefly and calmly explain. But you do not enter an argument and you do not back down. Just state your decision, and then decline to be drawn further. The teenager needs to see that the impact is real – and that feelings are not bargained away. Let's be clear: This is not how equal adults would behave towards each other. But you are a *parent* and you are doing relationship education – and you are combining this with teaching consequences to actions in your home.

What if she doesn't come back and ask for something?

No problem. Just wait till the next day and calmly explain, as Mum did above, about the behaviours. Then choose what you feel is a fair withdrawal of one of your services.

> Mum (next morning): 'Ally – you were really rude to me yesterday. Not just that – pretty disrespectful, too. That is hurtful, you know? So, I'm handing over my basketball duties to Dad tonight. I won't be going.'
>
> Ally: 'Whaat? But you can't. You know Dad is always late and he doesn't bring the snacks. It has to be you, he's just no good. Don't do this – I'm sorry, alright?'
>
> Mum: 'Sorry, love. Try again another time.'

For example:

Mum did the right thing. She shouldn't be wheedled or argued out of her feelings. That would have taught Ally that pressure makes people cave in – even when they don't feel okay about something.

There was no arguing, yelling, following, or grounding by Mum. But don't you think that Ally will think twice next time she is rude?

What is really important is that you do *not* teach your teenagers that wrong behaviours are dealt with either:

1. following, shouting and escalating
2. un-questioning absorption of the hurtful actions

The first of these is modelling something close to domestic violence – and the second, modelling an intimidated individual's acceptance of the same. Instead, you can teach your kids that:

1. People don't have to 'react in the moment'
2. You can stay quiet and think
3. You can be thoughtful in your response
4. But be resolved and firm
5. Nasty behaviour to another does have consequences
6. No-one needs to be pushed around – or to do the pushing

If you feel you are stumped about suitable consequences, here is another useful thing to remember: while teenagers are great at power behaviours and throwing around insults, they are maybe not such independent people after all. They need you for more than they care to realise.

Have a think about it. You probably provide:

- A comfortable room
- Nice dinners (not just 'food')
- Transport to and from school
- Transport/equipment/fees for their sports activities
- Money for parties/outings
- TV
- Money for gifts for their friends
- Occasional takeaways
- Trips to the mall and movies
- More devices than you can poke a stick at
- Extra clothes
- Help with their leisure activities
- A lot of driving around

- ❖ Welcoming their friends to your home
- ❖ Help with their homework and projects
- ❖ Advocacy to their teachers
- ❖ General help, advice and assistance
- ❖ Allowing trips and sleepovers

… There's a lot more room in all of those for appropriate consequences, than just the same old 'grounding' and 'taking your screens away'.

If parents do resort to repeatedly using grounding and the removal of devices, teens usually respond with a combination of these lovely things:

- ❖ Sullenness
- ❖ Boredom
- ❖ Indifference
- ❖ Having something to complain to their friends about, which reinforces an attitude of negativity towards you
- ❖ A feeling that they shouldn't have to co-operate with you because you are so mean and unfair
- ❖ A secret feeling that their parents are 'dumb' for being so un-imaginative

Replace those with something that is fair but more imaginative and real, and the platform for those negativities instantly vanishes.

REMINDERS

Try and remember our latest Golden Rule when you are confronted with 'awful' teenage behaviours:

Golden Rule #4

Remember that these types of behaviours are happening in hundreds of houses in your suburb! They are not an emergency and you have got this. Therefore:

DO NOT FEEL HURT.

Try and practice our first set of BEHAVIOUR SUPPORT PRINCIPLES:

1. You don't have to respond in the moment. You can wait for hours and sometimes days.
2. You don't have to provide a consistent (i.e., predictable) response.
3. You must be fair at all times.

And remember to teach that....

1. People don't have to react in the moment
2. You can stay quiet and think
3. You can be thoughtful in your response
4. But be resolved and firm
5. Nasty behaviour to another does have consequences
6. No-one needs to be pushed around – or to do the pushing

CHAPTER 11

RULES FOR DEALING WITH THE BEHAVIOURS

Our Vulnerable Emotional Touch-Points

Just as babies arrive designed to cry at just the right pitch to make a parent leap into action (oh – who can ignore that very special brand of noise?), teenagers are equipped with thrilling accoutrements of their own, which are closely allied to the Big Red Hot Button. Yes! They can...

- ❖ Repeatedly not do their homework and then slope off somewhere
- ❖ Show horrifying rudeness at a family event in front of everyone
- ❖ Show an amazing level of contempt when you've just spent your last money and all of your energy on something for them

These are indeed sophisticated pieces of (faulty) emotional equipment. Unfortunately, these talents do have impacts on their adult family members – and not exactly of the helpful variety. Here are some of the words that parents have used to describe the impacts that they feel:

❖ Mad. Mad as anything….

❖ Stupid. What am I supposed to do?

❖ Confused. Do I let it go, or come down on the behaviour hard?

❖ Like they are in control, not me

❖ Like my life's not my own any more

❖ Like I don't have a say in my own house

❖ Like they just don't care about me at all

❖ Is it worth it?

❖ I feel totally ineffective

❖ We are demoralised

I think that parents feel disturbed when they think they are doing badly and they don't have answers. But actually, this is only a cultural overlay. Imagine instead that we feel the exact opposite – that is, that we know what this is all about, and how to deal with it.

Here is what might happen in a forest-dwelling tribe from another planet. They view knotty teenaged behaviours through a lens of sympathetic amusement, logically concluding that they are merely the result of teenagers being people who are not fully developed yet.

Alien Dad: 'I fixed up that canoe for him specially but he didn't come and use it – for about the fourth time.'

Dad's Auntie: 'Ah, yes, that's funny dear! That's Immaturity number 17.'

Dad: 'Aha. Pass the cookies. I know what to do with number 17.'

Sounds peaceful. However, *you also* may be able to unhook yourself from the teenagers' emotional effects if:

1. You can detach yourself from the damage that you feel has been done to your relationship with your child.

2. Put yourself into emotional neutral for a couple of weeks, take stock of which developmental supports you feel that your child needs in their life – then start putting into action helpful techniques for responding to challenging behaviours. The chances are that you will end up feeling a whole lot more positive about your child and the way things can work in your house.

Island living, anyone?

Using the following will be very important. This comprises:

PARENTAL LEADERSHIP

❖ Cool and confident parenting

❖ Thinking very carefully before we respond

❖ Modelling respectful speech

- ❖ Modelling respectful and confident conflict management

- ❖ Modelling mutual support between the adults – with no-one being taken for granted

- ❖ Slowing firm and consistent boundaries

- ❖ Keeping our word

- ❖ Listening

- ❖ Making a strong family culture

- ❖ Relating honestly

Teenagers have their own acute Truth Radar. If you try and insist on them behaving in ways that you yourself can't manage, your credibility with them will be zero.

The list above might look like a big To Do list. But if you use the principles described below you are likely to feel rather more confident, and as if it could actually work for you.

BEHAVIOUR SUPPORT PRINCIPLES

❖ With teenagers, you don't have to respond right at that moment – in fact, it is often better not to (just as in your own adult relationships)

❖ Give yourself time to calm right down

❖ Wait until the 'right' moment and be inspired to have the 'right' (i.e., emotionally true) response

❖ You do not have to be entirely predictable in your responses, but you must be fair

❖ Do not escalate

❖ Do not yell. Do not use insults, comparisons, or put-downs

❖ Do not make empty threats (this makes your word worth nothing). In fact – do not make any threats

❖ Instead, use real-world consequences (trying to shield them from these only perpetuates immaturity)

❖ Sometimes, humour is the best remedy!

When can you use humour?

Only once you have begun to establish your new responses, and your teen has got used to them (that's only fair). Do NOT use humour if there is someone else present, or if there is a behaviour happening which is directed at another person (that is likely to be disrespectful to someone else). But you can use it (sometimes) if you and your teenager are alone, and if the behaviour is at a low-level.

For example:

Teenager: '(Mumble, mumble...) ...you can't *make* me, you know. Your rules are dumb.' (Begins to leave).

Mum: 'I heard that. Poor effort. That's only a 2 out of 10 for rudeness, Joshua!'

Teenager: 'Whaa?' (Later heard laughing sheepishly).

Since he has registered your point and you are both in good humour, nothing further is needed. Save your carefully targeted responses for the behaviours which merit it.

REMINDERS

❖ Remember to recover – by putting yourself into *emotional neutral* and taking stock of which developmental supports your child needs.

❖ Show Parental Leadership (p.148)

❖ And use the Behaviour Support Principles (p.150)

CHAPTER 12

WHEN BEHAVIOURS COME IN GROUPS

It's great to have techniques to deal with poor teenage behaviours more easily, but if you have picked up this book then you may be experiencing more than just sporadic troubles. Acting-out behaviours often clump together into groups. We can look at each of these groups to see what helps – assuming for the moment, that the groups themselves have not yet joined up to produce a teen who does everything on the list.

Note: If you do have a teenager who is showing *all* of the behaviours from the list on page 129, this would feel like a pervasive problem. It is more likely to mean that:

a) their general adjustment is poor; and
b) that that the relationships within the house have deteriorated quite dramatically.

You may need a professional's assessment to assist with a situation which has developed to this level of hostility.

GROUP 1: RUDENESS

> **GROUP 1 FEATURES:**
>
> ❖ Rudeness
>
> ❖ Disrespect (often followed by walking out or walking away)
>
> ❖ Being scathing

Teenagers often forget themselves or use words in a way that just let their emotions out. They are unlikely to understand the consequences for other people – so it's our job to teach them. Don't forget that there is an awful lot of modelling for this out in the world: at school in peer groups, in music videos, on YouTube, on TV shows, on buses… You will be teaching them that their words matter, and other people's feelings matter. And you'll be doing this in a way which doesn't raise the temperature or cause further conflict. See page 145 above for the basic approach to this group of behaviours.

Teens in this group, like all of those with behaviours described in this section, are showing us that there are gaps in their knowledge: there are things they don't get yet. No matter how haughty they might appear, or how superior their arguments are, they are acting blindly. This is different to when there are mental health issues or an abusive dynamic within their home – then acting out can become an unavoidable expression of discomfort.

This is what young people who are being rude need to learn:

❖ Everything that comes out of our mouth, matters: once out, you can't credibly take it back.

❖ It is our responsibility to learn to speak to others tolerably well, even if we are feeling difficult emotions.

❖ People rely on us for feeling emotionally safe near us.

❖ Our rudeness affects others in the house – not just the person we are speaking to.

❖ It's like throwing a rock in a pond – people within earshot either have to try and tune this out (and then they feel complicit) – or else get involved, and then they'll get shouted at and accused.

❖ Rudeness which goes on for any length of time is corrosive to a relationship. A teenager is unlikely to understand this. Often fairly egocentric, their emotions take over when they feel strongly, and the first thing to go out of the window is insight. But a mother, for example, who has been on the receiving end of rudeness from a teen will either not notice it (Red light! This is the thin end of the wedge for tolerating domestic abuse) – or they will feel hurt and resentful inside, and their warmth towards their child will be progressively reducing as we speak.

All of this means that it is important to address. The 'Rude' teenager is acting on the basis of ignorance, and the parent – or sibling – on the receiving end is getting hurt, and the teen is about to lose the other person's goodwill altogether. What can we do? The first thing is to never mention the points above to the person while they are in the middle of a tirade. You are on a guaranteed losing path if you try this one! Instead, set your goals clearly for your child and what is appropriate to their age level. Have clearly in mind the concept that you would like them to learn (see above). Then find a way to teach these to them – a very small piece at a time. And – do this at a time when there is no (or only low) tension in the house. Once you have explained these ideas to your child, you can remind them gently when they forget themselves – IF the rudeness is just starting. Once they are in full flight – it is too late.

Thomas is 15 and he has taken part in conversations about keeping a cordial space around people. But he's starting again…

'Why do you nag me so much? You should be in a nagging competition. Nag, nag, nag. I'll….'

Mum interrupts, quietly: 'Tom, your sister is right there on the sofa. Shall we take this somewhere else?' (Making good eye contact).

Tom pauses, and nods. They move into the next room.

Mum: 'Now love, what did you want to tell me?'

If your teenager takes off into the full package of rudeness and disrespect, follow **Golden Rule Number 1** and disengage from them. If you have already had the conversation about the rules here, you can then approach them later when things are calm and quiet, to briefly point out how the rudeness affected you and remind what you have all agreed.

GROUP 2: PASSIVE-AGGRESSION

Some people might feel that this group of annoying behaviours are just 'what's typical for teenagers'. But do we want them to be? Surely, the young person would show anything but these when they are at their evening job, at their girlfriend's house, or trying to impress their coach at their favourite sporting event. So here is the key: if they show motivated behaviours in other environments, they are able to show these at home. And if they cannot show motivated or engaged behaviours *anywhere* – there is something more profoundly wrong and someone needs to find out what is troubling the child enough to start sending them down an anti-social track. However, teenagers have a particular vulnerability to inertia, that is: a lack of action. They may believe that this is ok, and that it does not hurt anyone. If you overhear them speaking to their friends about this, they are likely to be saying, 'Aaargh... I can't be bothered' (or words to that effect). Now it's funny, because when we see that inertia in younger children we usually have no problem at all in chivvying them and telling them why it's no good to be on the couch when they should be brushing the dog/ doing their homework/getting ready for a shower. We tend to tiptoe around our older children... maybe because we're afraid of explosions. Goodness! Who is in charge here?

We have found that a very helpful approach is to talk to your child about how they sometimes feel overwhelm or inertia. Ask them what it feels like, and when it mostly happens? You will need to explain that you can understand what they are saying – but that it is your role to teach them life skills which actually work (it is not your role as a parent to put tricky issues on the shelf). You can then outline to them what types of activity you expect from them in your household. Some of the tasks that you have in mind will have to be done then and there, but some of them may be able to wait. If you can work this out with your child, they will appreciate your flexibility and you will have set up a collaborative dialogue. Then, if you are observing the pattern of 'can't be bothered' again – you can sit down and have a quiet chat to remind them of what you talked about together. Try to agree when they can do what is being asked (and remember – this is a very important training ground for adult life – a future boss won't wait until someone can be bothered!).

If the teenager can't manage this... then it may be time to explain that some things in your house are earned by co-operation, and so they won't be available until they have done their part.

Above all – avoid being drawn into a pattern of nagging repeatedly or arguing with your child... once you have tipped into this position, they will feel they can legitimately feel oppositional towards you.

GROUP 3: AVOIDANCE OF LEARNING

GROUP 3 FEATURES:

❖ Failure to do schoolwork

❖ Trying not to attend school

These are often an escalation of Group 2 behaviours. However, they can also signal other issues. For example, our school environment has changed a great deal and students are now expected to engage with a relatively limited number of subjects, mostly taught within a classic classroom environment involving the study of text alongside reading and writing... for long periods of time. There is not much diversity and often not much to enthral students who have little interest in the subject at hand. For example, 'real science' is often not taught in Australian schools until at least Year 9. This can be very annoying for kids who are itching to learn about the eccentric and fascinating way the universe works, in investigative ways (fun, because these experiments carry lots of surprises!).

Even worse, our near-universal focus on text-based teaching is hard to take for those who are better suited to outdoor or hands-on types of learning. No longer offered the option of trade or agricultural school, these kids may find that they have struggles with some areas of verbal learning (i.e., grammar, spelling, or verbal memory) and they feel quite uncomfortable trying to engage with this for long stretches. They may feel 'stupid' or become demoralised by observing that 'no-one else' is struggling as they are. And they are teenagers. Remember, it is vital for them to keep up their image to their peers, and to guard their self-esteem. So – if any of these issues are a problem, they may be causing the dreaded Drop-Out Effect – that is, they can be tempted to drop out of school rather than let their friends see that academic learning is a struggle. Try to investigate this collaboratively with your child. Review the pattern of past school reports and try to see if there are particular areas of struggle. If there really are, the child deserves some extra support. Cognitive testing will point out problem areas for children's learning very quickly – this is done by educational psychologists. If, on the other hand, the child is merely a slightly lower-level learner who is not terribly interested in academic subjects (and again, there is often very little choice before the Year 10 Level), you may need to agree with their expectations for how much work they put in, and how this can be balanced by offering them opportunities to learn something they would really enjoy.

GROUP 4A FEATURES:

❖ Arguing back

❖ Escalating situations very quickly

GROUP 4A): OPPOSITION

In the Group 4a behaviours, we are beginning to see aggression and a willingness to take it to the next level. What is behind this? The answer is that there is no one single cause – but many possible ones, often combined together. For example, if a person in their teens is beginning to openly argue back to you, contributing factors could be:

- ❖ In their home there are frequent arguments and people yelling at each other
- ❖ They do not feel respected by you
- ❖ They do not feel listened to by you
- ❖ They do not like what is going on in their family

But perhaps, more commonly, there may be a combination that:

- ❖ They have not been stopped from doing this in previous years
- ❖ Parents have tended to escalate to arguments when the child has previously talked back (so they are actually copying you)
- ❖ They hear tales of dissatisfaction from friends about their families
- ❖ They hear exaggerated stories of how one of their friends 'told it like it is'… and got away with it
- ❖ They are not in control of their emotions – and no-one in their family has yet sat down and talked through this with them in a calm and meaningful way
- ❖ The common 'teenaged sense of entitlement' that we talk about so often is beginning to become evident
- ❖ They do not appreciate the damaging impact of speaking in this way

A useful approach is to bear these possible factors in mind, and with this clarity, talk to your child at a time when tension is low. Without being punitive, explain that those behaviours are very damaging within your home and you will both need to work on preventing them. ASK what triggers or provocations the teenager feels are at play. They might come up with something you did not realise was a problem in your house. On the other hand, automatic blaming of everyone-but-themselves is just a sign of poor insight.

Armed with your new knowledge, you will begin to see a way forward. If emotion-regulation is a problem for your child, you will need to support them with agreed approaches to help them re-shape this experience. This takes time, but often, children respond very well once they understand the issue and are given a combination of enough space with some firm boundaries around that space, to take actions to calm themselves down. For example, it isn't helpful to react to every misstep that your child makes. Instead, let minor transgression go (maybe raise an eyebrow) – and remind them of your plans for them to take space and calm down if it goes up a notch. If they get to the stage where things become nasty, do not yell, admonish, or try to reason with them. Merely back away and – as in the prior chapters – deal with it later, very calmly, but remember to hold the line with what you have agreed. People who have the characteristics enabling them to push boundaries often follow up by testing your resolve to hold them!

In regard to escalation, this often involves a combination of feeling caught up with emotions – being unaware that this has an impact on others… and a certain amount of hostility also.

> ### GROUP 4B FEATURES:
>
> ❖ Contempt
>
> ❖ Threats
>
> ❖ Verbal aggression or verbal attack

GROUP 4B): HOSTILITY

We can certainly see how 4a can easily lead to Group 4b: either as emotional dysregulation increases and/or nobody effectively reins it in; or as some kind or perceived or real dissatisfaction felt by the teenager becomes more and more marked.

Group 4b behaviours comprise a serious situation and these often cause high tension in a household – or in a sole parent household, absolute despair. Don't forget that professional help is available if it feels beyond your capacity to unravel the reasons underneath these reactions, or if you need help with maintaining your calm and teaching your teen appropriate social conduct.

Sometimes it is very hard to negotiate the margin between feeling like a doormat and absorbing or letting the behaviours go on the one hand; and yelling, following, and threatening on the other. In the middle lies calmness, planned responses, and the knowledge that you are able to communicate your family rules and your hopes for your child, directly to the volatile young person. You will need to be in a position where you have confidence in yourself to draw the line with their unskilful and dysregulated behaviours, while teaching your child the emotional and social skills they will need in the world... for the rest of their lives.

GROUP 5: DISREGARD FOR SIBLINGS

> **GROUP 5 FEATURES:**
>
> ❖ Disregard or lack of co-operation with siblings

Group 5 behaviours are basically a failure of empathy in an older child and/or a failure to see their own needs as fitting into the entire landscape, where everyone's needs and wants are at play. In a teenager, this is actually more serious than it looks. This is because either:

a) Your family environment has failed to teach them these skills over the past several years, or;

b) Others in the family are modelling and teaching a lack of respect and contempt for others, or;

c) The child has a developmental issue which is delaying the development of these crucial processing skills

If your child has a consistent pattern both at home and with peers of poorly understanding social interactions, lacking in empathy, or not being able to support others' agendas, they may need screening for issues such as autism spectrum or social processing disorders.

If you do not feel this is the case, then you need to start from scratch in helping them to develop empathy and an appreciation of how everyone's needs fit together. Additionally, they will need their understanding of respect

– for themselves and others – to be built up properly. This is not a quick fix. However, if you are able to catch these issues now, and intervene to help your child work co-operatively, sympathetically and assertively in the world, you will be doing them an enormous favour.

GROUP 6: RULE-BREAKING

GROUP 6 FEATURES:

❖ Boundary-breaking

❖ Lying

❖ Minor stealing

Group no. 6 is an interesting group of behaviours – and a worrying one. A crucial question to ask is whether the child has always tended to respond this way when they feel hemmed in or they want something, or if it is more recent.

If these behaviours have been around forever, then the person's insight into why they are concerning is likely to be low. Additionally, they themselves might think (or say): 'What's the big deal?' – as they have been feeling this way for as long as they can remember. The big deal *now*, though, is that at their more advanced age and with greater knowledge about the world and ability to navigate within it, these behaviours put them at increased risk in all sorts of ways.

If the behaviours are recent, they might be influenced by a peer group who brag about this stuff; or they might be arising from resentment or a sudden feeling that 'Grownups are all c**p and none of what they say matters'. Either way, they are a warning sign. Telling-off and yelling aren't going to get very far with someone who has begun to experience a thrill from breaking family and social conventions.

One thing NOT to do is to fall into the trap of assuring your child that you 'trust them'. Because – do you?

Here is a conversation where a dad engages with his son – who has taken $50 meant for an excursion and spent it on gaming equipment. And it's not the first time that his parents have found that some of their money is missing.

Dad: 'I've just heard from Mr Mason, and you didn't arrive for the excursion to the Science Museum. And they didn't receive the money for it. I found this (holds up the games pack) in your room and it's still got the price sticker on it – $49.95. I'm afraid that you took the $50, and Jesse – it's not the first time you've taken money from Mum and me.'

Jesse: 'What? No I didn't. Mr Mason has it wrong. Actually, he's a fool. Ask Paulie – that excursion was cancelled but Mr Mason just didn't realise.'

Dad: 'I have already talked to Paulie and Steve's mother. They went on the excursion on Friday.'

Jesse: 'What the f**k. Alright. It was a worthless trip and I didn't want to go. It was stupid them thinking we all should go when I hate science, anyway. It's only $50. It's not as if you guys will miss that.'

Dad: 'I don't know if you realised, but lately Mum has been limiting herself to two coffees out a week, and not buying any lunches at work, and she has even been cutting her own hair. Things are actually pretty tight since my work got downscaled. I'm surprised that you haven't noticed. So – we're going to have to change some things until we feel that you have understood how we all need to be trustworthy to each other. The first thing is, that we can't let you go fishing with Paulie and Steve this weekend. And we won't be letting you go off to the mall after school at the moment – we will be picking you up when your classes finish.'

Jesse: 'Huh? That's outrageous. All for a lousy $50. What's the matter, don't you trust me? I'm your own son, remember. I'm 16. You can't treat me like this.'

Dad: 'I love you, for sure, but trust isn't actually a word I'd use right now. How it works is that you will have to earn it back from both Mum and me. And it's going to take a while. We need to be a healthy functioning family and that means we have to be able to depend on each other. I will help you, but I need to feel that you get this.'

Jesse: *Stands there stunned and then walks away, swearing.*

This dad stood his ground and showed great presence of mind. He didn't lose his temper and he didn't get diverted by the disrespect and provocation. He also didn't fall into the trap of protesting (as many parents do): '*Of course* I trust you, it's just that...'

He outlined the consequences (which seem pretty fair) and re-iterated that Jesse had his love and would receive help. It is staggering, but not uncommon, that Jesse had not noticed that his parents were in financial strife and were bending over backwards to still give him everything they could (excursions, fishing trips). Maybe they need to do a little more to (carefully) let Jesse know what is going on and ensure that his empathy and sense of family is fully activated.

This is the type of action which helps with boundary-breaking behaviours.

DEALING WITH BOUNDARY-BREAKING

- ❖ Confront the issue calmly

- ❖ Know what you want to say

- ❖ Know what you WILL NOT be drawn into saying/ doing

- ❖ Don't get diverted

- ❖ Outline the consequences

- ❖ Re-iterate your support and the fact that you will help

- ❖ Be firm about what you want at the end of the learning process

- ❖ Set limits in the meantime

The consequences of NOT doing anything in this kind of situation are very real. The behaviours will escalate, your teenager's level of respect will keep on shrinking, and they will feel more and more emboldened to operate in this way. Most teenagers love adrenaline, remember?

One more thing. If your child's behaviours have progressed beyond the level described in this chapter, your family needs to call in professional help. Self-help only succeeds if you have some solid ground beneath your feet.

REMINDERS

Each behaviour group requires a slightly different approach – be targeted in how you deal with these problems

Remember not to fall into the trap of arguing about 'trust'

CHAPTER 13

WHEN THERE IS A 'WHOLE SITUATION'

As well as behaviours coming along in groups, situations can develop in a family where you are either faced with something new or something that feels like a whole mess that has gotten out of hand. When this happens it is very helpful to analyse the factors which are contributing to the root of the acting-out behaviours. When you feel satisfied that you've done this you can decide how you will try to manage the behavioural components as well.

Justine

Thirteen-year-old Justine has been in high school for two terms. She has always been rather volatile in her temperament – much more prone to losing her temper than her younger sister. Always an affectionate child, she could previously be relied on to show love and respect to both of her parents. Anna and Brent married young and have worked hard. They take pride in their home environment and have been alarmed to see

Justine's behaviours escalating. It's upsetting. Recently, it has reached the point where she screams loudly if she is told 'No'.

She has had outbursts of rudeness towards her mother, sometimes using some choice words! She is accusatory if things don't go her way and constantly wants to argue back. This often escalates into a yelling match. Anna and Brent feel as though their home life has changed drastically.

Anna and Brent decided to get the situation checked out by a child psychologist to start with. What if Justine was being bullied at the new school, or if she was suffering from depression? Neither of those concerns seemed to match. But here is what Brent, Anna, and the psychologist thought was relevant:

- ❖ The culture change of high school had thrown Justine. Her new friends talked about how they 'wouldn't take any garbage' from their parents and boasted about retaliation if they were thwarted at home.
- ❖ Social media use had taken off to a whole new level amongst Justine's friend group. Justine had confusing things to keep up with that she had not encountered before.
- ❖ Her routine had completely changed.
- ❖ Hormones seemed to be playing a part – Justine was developing physically.
- ❖ The close structure of primary school – with tightly knit groups of friends and their families, and well-

known teachers who were able to supervise closely, had melted away.

❖ Justine's original temperament was still relevant.

Seen in this light, Justine's behaviours made logical sense. Anna felt very relieved. She had taken the changes to her little girl very hard, feeling bewildered and even betrayed that her daughter had changed from a 'mummy's girl', to an acerbic teen constantly launching personal attacks. The psychologist helped the family to make a plan:

❖ A longer-term plan was made to help Justine with her pattern of emotional volatility. This had been in the background for a long time and Justine needed to learn emotional self-regulation. If she had reached the mid-teenage years without this, both she and her parents would have been in for a confusing and rough ride.

❖ Brent and Anna explained to both of the girls what kinds of behaviours they preferred to see in their home and what would be unacceptable: yelling at people, put-downs, insults, deliberate rudeness. These would garner consequences. Overall, they would like their house to be a nice place for everyone.

❖ Anna and Brent felt less tense and so they promoted a calm mood in the house, and they showed more affection to each other again.

❖ When Justine tried to escalate situations or cause long exchanges with answering back, they did not bite. Instead, they would briefly re-state their requirements and then turn away. If she tried to follow, they would melt away into the garage, seem to need the bathroom, or suddenly make a phone call. Justine gained no negative traction here.

❖ Screen time was radically re-organised: strict boundaries were set upon the times of usage and the types of social media Justine could access.

❖ If Justine had not completed a chore, she was given a consequence.

❖ Anna and Brent dealt with the rudeness and yelling with relationship-based techniques, letting her know that they could not bake cookies with her or take her for a play date after what had happened.

Suddenly, things changed. After just one week, Anna sent a photo of herself with a big smile to the psychologist with the caption 'IT WORKS!' The psychologist was very pleased for the family, and further plans were made to tackle Justine's temperament vulnerabilities.

Can this be right? How come it worked so quickly? Yes, it can. This happens to be a true story. But it should be noted that this family had some big advantages to start with, so let's look at what these were:

❖ Justine and her sister have had a stable home life with good family and community connections.

❖ Their parents' relationship is a happy one and they usually deal with conflict well.

❖ The girls are well-socialised and both have a range of interests.

❖ Their history of friendships at school have been good.

> ❖ The family are warm towards each other and love doing things together.
>
> ❖ Anna and Brent talk things over and make joint decisions – they never undermine each other.

This explains why Anna and Brent didn't have to do much with the basic structure of the children's lives – this was already there. So all that was needed were relationship and behavioural techniques and the tightening up of some boundaries.

If you are thinking that that's nothing like your situation, don't despair. Much more complex configurations can be dealt with – but it takes more time and probably adding some of the Strengtheners for children that we have talked about earlier.

Let's have a look at Paolo.

Paolo

Paolo (14) is living in a situation with 50/50 access to his mother and father. He'd been a bright little button at primary school (before his parents' divorce) but had always had trouble settling to tasks and would wander around the classroom. As a young child, he had loved animals, spending hours in the garden examining bugs and attempting to train his pet lizards to do tricks. But all that has now changed. Now he hates school and does everything to avoid learning tasks; his mood is often poor. He has 'explosions' and can be very rude.

He is surly and shuts himself in his room 24/7 with his laptop and phone. He refuses to do any chores and most of his verbal exchanges are rude. He has no friends (except online) and will not do any homework. Now in Term 3, he is solidly refusing to go to school and has missed 50% of the term so far. His eating has declined and he constantly tries to insist on only having junk food. If his mother Patsy tries to discipline him he yells, swears prolifically at her and then runs down the drive, calling his father Tony to come and get him – which he does.

Patsy and Tony are always on the phone arguing: Patsy advocates for joint rules and boundaries to be implemented and she also feels that they need external help. Tony says he is concerned about nothing and Paolo is fine when at his house. He did admit that he allows unlimited screen access and that he does not monitor the content. He says that he "doesn't push it" if Paolo will not go to school, and that he "just gives Paolo whatever he wants to eat – at least it gets him eating."

Patsy is very worried about where this is all going.

❖ Patsy and Tony do not agree about how to set boundaries for Paolo – or how to intervene with him.

❖ He is subject to two different sets of rules and practices in two houses.

❖ His parents do not have a good relationship – even at a distance.

❖ This comes at a time when things are not going well for him and he is also full of teenage bluster!

❖ He does not have 'real' friendships to draw upon.

❖ At the moment, he seems to have no compensatory hobbies or interests.

❖ There seems to be something awry with his learning.

❖ His emotional state is poor.

Paolo's situation has more vulnerability factors.
These were the actions which helped Paolo:

❖ Paolo's school principal got in touch and arranged a meeting which included both parents. At the meeting a thorough psychological screen was agreed upon.

❖ The psychologist found that Paolo was experiencing ADHD to a significant level. This had been interfering with his ability to settle and learn in the classroom. He was also found to have some specific learning difficulties in the area of text-based processing.

❖ Patsy and Tony agreed to see a family counsellor. They felt mortified that Paolo had been dealing with his classroom struggles on his own for so long. Eventually, they were able to agree to much more consistent rules and practices. That included a drastic reduction in screen time.

❖ After a few months, Patsy and Tony decided to move Paolo away from his high-functioning and strongly academic school as they felt it had been affecting his self-esteem. He moved to a school with a diverse curriculum and plenty of outdoor activities.

❖ Patsy has a friend who trains horses. He was delighted to take on a helper and Paolo became intrigued by the processes used to guide and train the young horses. He spent more and more time over there at weekends.

❖ Eight months later, Patsy and Tony realised that their son was often smiling; he bounced around the house energetically (even on his new medication) and he loved his outdoor pursuits. He had begun to talk about following in the footsteps of his new mentor.

Jackson

Jackson (16) is living with his mother, Annalise, and younger brother, Cal, in government housing. Annalise is on a disability pension after a back injury at work.

Annalise has often felt that Jackson can be 'too much for her'. She has also struggled to keep up with the expenses of raising two children: school excursions, laptops, and sports activities outside of school.

Jackson has been speaking to Annalise and Cal with more and more contempt. He is disengaging with school and often comes home several hours late. He refuses to say where he has been but Mum is aware that drugs are a currency in his friendship group. Jackson has started to refuse co-operation with anything that his mother asks and last week he threw two cups on the floor and smashed them during an argument. Annalise feels mortified that she had to withdraw Jackson from basketball due to financial constraints: for a long time this had been his only outlet. He keeps asking to start learning to drive but Annalise has no car.

Jackson's school was in touch last week to ask about several days when he had not arrived.

Jackson's situation will become an emergency if his family does not get help soon:

❖ Jackson does not have an easy temperament and Annalise has no-one else to step in and help.

❖ He is showing that he is disengaging with school and also with this family.

❖ He is drifting towards a powerful friend group which is influencing him to disappear from home and school and experiment with drugs.

- ❖ He has lost his much-loved connection with basketball – which had been, for a long time, a strong positive in his life.

- ❖ He is showing poor community engagement and a desire to cope by showing power and control.

- ❖ At present, his family has poor access to resources.

Here's what happened:

- ❖ The school counsellor arranged some meetings with Jackson. She found that he was angry and disillusioned and he thought little of his own abilities. Cognitive testing showed that he had a learning profile not best suited to academic-style pursuits. The counsellor went through some course alternative with Jackson and he showed a strong interest in mechanics.
- ❖ Jackson was transferred to a vocational learning stream where he was allowed block-release to college twice a week.
- ❖ The school counsellor linked Jackson to a male mentor who had strong involvement in basketball. After listening to Jackson, the mentor contacted a colleague in a welfare organisation who provided a sports grant for Jackson to re-join his basketball team.
- ❖ The school counsellor met with Jackson and Annalise to help them to repair their relationship.

❖ There was huge relief all around when the auto-mechanics teacher at college provided positive feedback on Jackson's progress. He also mentioned that a government scheme could help in teaching Jackson to drive.

Jackson had needed a clear assessment of his issues and major adjustments to his learning pathway. As Annalise had suspected, he needed more resources than she could offer. Regaining his beloved sport and with more men around to help him, it began to look as though Jackson was finding his own place in the world.

Very often if we can assist early enough, a lot can change. Where many aspects are going wrong for a teenager (and look how good they are at showing us!), a thorough assessment of the whole situation is a must. Crucially, different types of support may then be necessary to help the multiple elements which are not working. The more a situation deteriorates the more external help the family is likely to need.

Don't delay if you feel that there is a whole situation developing for your child. There are often resources available that you haven't yet heard of. Your main task may be to ask for help – and keep asking until you feel that every aspect has been addressed.

REMINDERS

When there is a whole situation, there are likely to be several contributing factors.

Often, these need the assistance of other professionals to analyse them all.

All of them will need to be actioned. If they are not, it will become an explosive partial fix.

CHAPTER 14

ENCOURAGEMENT

With your help, this book has taken a detailed look at some of the most worrying behaviours that our teenagers present with… and what lies underneath them. We've examined what produces vulnerability and damage to healthy development, and surveyed techniques to repair and strengthen the young person and their path forward in life. And now it's over to you. Whether your home is in Toorak or Turramurra, and whether you have a supportive extended family or no-one at all, you can make an enormous difference to the culture of your family. By using balance and a breadth of techniques, it is almost always possible to improve your relationship with your teen and the confidence that you have in each other.

You may not always be able to do this without a little help along the way. There is nothing wrong with that: raising young people requires more on-the-hoof judgement than the paid work that most of us will ever do. Here are some organisations which you may find helpful.

RESOURCES

The Alcohol and Drug Foundation
www.adf.org.au

Asperger Syndrome Support Network
www.aspergersvic.org.au

Australian Childhood Foundation: Counselling for children and young people affected by abuse
www.childhood.org.au
Ph: 1800 176 453

Australian Health Practitioner Regulation Agency (AHPRA) – Australia's regulatory agency for health professionals
www.ahpra.gov.au

Australian Psychological Society (APS)
www.psychology.org.au

Autism Awareness Australia
www.autismawareness.com.au

Beyond Blue – Support and advice for depression and mental health concerns
www.beyondblue.org.au www.healthyfamilies.beyondblue.org.au

Black Dog Institute – Information links and advice for depression and mental health concerns
www.blackdoginstitute.org.au

Child and Adolescent Mental Health Services
NSW: (02) 9391 9000
NT: (08) 8999 4959
SA: 1300 2 CAMHS (1300 222 647)
TAS: (03) 6777 2277
VIC: 1300 721 927
WA: (08) 6389 5800

Child and Youth Mental Health Services
QLD: (07) 3068 2555

Department of Health and Human Services
VIC: 1300 650 172

Department of Health and Human Services Child Protection Intake
QLD: (07) 3235 9999
NSW: 13 21 11
NT: 1800 700 250
SA: 13 14 78
TAS: 1300 737 639
VIC (North): 1300 664 977
VIC (South): 1300 655 795
VIC (East): 1300 360 391
VIC (West – Rural): 1800 075 599
VIC (West – Metro): 1300 664 977
VIC (After Hours): 13 12 78
WA: (08) 9325 1111

eSafety Commissioner – Government website with information for online safety
www.esafety.gov.au

Family Violence Law Help – A national website for people wanting to understand the law related to domestic and family violence, family court proceedings, and child protection
www.familyviolencelaw.gov.au

Headspace – Treatment resources for young people with mental health concerns
www.headspace.org.au

Kids Help Line – Telephone counselling for children and young people
Ph: 1800 551 800
www.kidshelp.com.au

Lifeline – Telephone assistance for those in need of mental health support
Ph: 13 11 14

National Sexual Assault, Family and Domestic Violence Counselling Line – First point of call for access to all services across Australia (24 hours a day)
Ph: 1800 737 732
www.1800respect.org.au

The Orange Door – a free service for adults, children and young people who are victims of family violence and families who need extra support with the care of children
www.orangedoor.vic.gov.au

Raise – a mentoring organisation for teenagers
www.raise.org.au

Raising Children (Teens) – Tips and links for raising teenagers
www.raisingchildren.net.au/teens

The Smith Family – assistance for disadvantaged children with learning pathways
www.thesmithfamily.com.au

Safe Steps Domestic Violence Service – Family Violence Response
Centre
Ph: 1800 015 188

Women's Legal Services – National network of community legal
centres specialising in women's legal issues providing advice,
information, casework, and legal education to women.
www.wlsa.org.au/member

BIBLIOGRAPHY

[1] Bobic N. 'Adolescent violence towards parents', *Australian Domestic and Family Violence Clearinghouse Topic Paper*. 2004.

[2] Moulds L, Day A, Mayshak R, Mildred H, Miller P. 'Adolescent violence towards parents – prevalence and characteristics using Australian Police data', *Australian and New Zealand Journal of Criminology*. 2018; 52(2).

[3] Australian Bureau of Statistics. 2016-17 Apparent Consumption of Alcohol Report. [Internet] Canberra, ACT: Australian Bureau of Statistics 2018 Sept; accessed July 2021. https://www.abs.gov.au/AUSSTATS/abs@.nsf/Lookup/4307.0.55.001Main+Features12016-17?OpenDocument=

[4] Gates L. 'ABS Director of Health Statistics in Media Release in relation to the 2016-17 Apparent consumption of alcohol report',. [Internet] Canberra, ACT: Australian Bureau of Statistics 2018 Sept: accessed July 2021. Available from:. https://www.abs.gov.au/ausstats/abs@.nsf/Previousproducts/4307.0.55.001Media%20Release12016-17?opendocument&tabname=Summary&prodno=4307.0.55.001&issue=2016-17&num=&view=

[5] Johnston LD, Miech RA, O'Malley PM, Bachman JE, Patrick ME. 'Monitoring the future national survey results on drug use 1975-2020: Overview, key findings on adolescent drug use,' Ann Arbor, Michigan: Institute of Social Research, University of Michigan 2020 Jan; accessed July 2021. https://eric.ed.gov/?id=ED604018

6 *The National Center for Safe Routes to School* [Website]. North Carolina: UNC Highway Safety Research Centre 2021; accessed September 2021. http://www.saferoutesinfo.org

7 Her Majesty's Government, Department for Transport. *National Travel Survey*. London: Her Majesty's Government 2018; accessed June 2020. https://www.gov.uk/government/statistics/national-travel-survey-2018

8 VicHealth. 'Health promotion foundation VicHealth is teaming up with local councils across Victoria to get more kids walking, riding and scooting to school with funding of up to $10,000 per year announced today', Melbourne (VIC): VicHealth March 2018; accessed July 2021. https://www.vichealth.vic.gov.au/media-and-resources/media-releases/new-funding-to-get-local-kids-walking-to-school

9 NCD Risk Factor Collaboration. 'Worldwide trends in body-mass index, underweight, overweight, and obesity from 1975 to 2016: a pooled analysis of 2416 population-based measurement studies in 128.9 million children, adolescents, and adults', *Lancet*. December 2017; 390(10113):2627-2642.

10 Ashleigh LM, Freedman D, Sherry B, Blanck HM. 'Obesity – United States, 1999-2010,' *MMRW Supplements*. Hyatsville MD: CDC, National Center for Chronic Disease Prevention and Health Promotion, Division of Nutrition, Physical Activity, and Obesity 2013 Nov; accessed September 2020. https://www.cdc.gov/mmwr/preview/mmwrhtml/su6203a20.htm

11 Department of Health. *Australia's Physical Activity and Sedentary Behaviour Guidelines*. Canberra, ACT: Commonwealth of Australia 2021 May; accessed September 2021. https://www.health.gov.au/health-topics/physical-activity-and-exercise/physical-activity-and-exercise-guidelines-for-all-australians

12 Lifestyles Team, NHS Digital. *Health survey for England 2018*. NHS; accessed March 2021. https://digital.nhs.uk/data-and-information/publications/statistical/health-survey-for-england/2018

13 Office for National Statistics. *Labour Market Overview, UK: June 2020*. London: Her Majesty's Government; accessed June 2021. https://www.ons.gov.uk/employmentandlabourmarket/peopleinwork/employmentandemployeetypes/bulletins/uklabourmarket/june2020

14 Office for National Statistics. *Female Employment Rate (aged 16 to 64, seasonally adjusted)*. London: Her Majesty's Government 2018; accessed March 2021. https://www.ons.gov.uk/employmentandlabourmarket/peopleinwork/employmentandemployeetypes/timeseries/lf25/lms

15 US Bureau of Labor Statistics. 'Labour force participation rate down, employment-population ratio little changed in September', *The Economics Daily*. US Bureau of Labor Statistics. Washington DC 2020 Oct; accessed September 2021. https://www.bls.gov/opub/ted/2020/labor-force-participation-rate-down-employment-population-ratio-little-changed-in-september.htm

16 Heitler S. 'High school and college student anxiety: why the epidemic? An inside look into the drastic rise in anxiety rates among students', *Psychology Today New York; 2018 Jun; accessed* July 2020. https://www.psychologytoday.com/au/blog/resolution-not-conflict/201806/high-school-and-college-student-anxiety-why-the-epidemic

17 Cullinane C. 'Tackling the "Shadow Education System"', *The Sutton Trust* 2019, Sept; accessed September 2020. https://www.suttontrust.com/news-opinion/all-news-opinion/tackling-the-shadow-education-system-private-tuition/

18 Gotcha4Life (Website), accessed 2020. https://www.gotcha4life.org

19 *Save our Mates*, [Website], accessed 2020. http://www.saveourmates.com.au

20 Kepanga M. 'In my tribe, we go to a different type of school', *UNESCO World Education Blog* 2016, Sept; accessed October 2020. https://gemreportunesco.wordpress.com/2016/09/15/in-my-tribe-we-go-to-a-different-type-of-school/

21 Diamond J. *The World Until Yesterday*. New York: Viking Press, 2012.

22 Meltzer A, Saunders I. 'Cultivating supportive communities for young people – Mentor pathways into and following a youth mentoring program', *Children and Youth Services Review* 2020;110:104815.

23 Sanchez B. 'Mentoring for black male youth', *National Mentoring Resource Centre Population Review*, National Mentoring Resource Centre 2016 Aug; accessed July 2020. http:// nationalmentoringresourcecenter.org/images/PDF/BlackMales_ Population_Review.pdf

24 Timpe ZC, Lunkenheimer E. 'The long-term economic benefits of natural mentoring relationships for youth', *American Journal of Community Psychology*, September 2015; 56(0):12–24.

25 Feldmen DB, Kravetz LD. *Supersurvivors: The Surprising Link between Suffering and Success*. New York: Harper Wave; 2014.

26 Snyder CR. 'Reality negotiation: from excuses to hope and beyond', Journal o*f Social and Clinical Psychology*. 1989;8(2):130–157.

27 Armstrong T. *Power of the Adolescent Brain*. Virginia: Association for Supervision and Curriculum Development; 2016.

28 Griffin A. 'Adolescent neurological development and implications for health and well-being', *Healthcare*. 2017 Sept;5(4):62.

29 Wise RA, Robbie MA. 'Dopamine and addiction,' *Annual Review of Psychology*. 2020;71:79–106.

30 Romeo RD. 'The teenage brain: the stress response and the adolescent brain', *Current Directions in Psychological Science*. 2013 Apr;22(2):140–145.